In the Enemy Camp . . .

Oliver squeezed the trigger. Flame shot from the barrel. In the confined space, the report was deafening.

Taken full in the chest with the bullet, Mr. Quist toppled backward and sprawled on the floor. But the self-satisfied smile never left his face. He lay quietly a few seconds, then drew one large breath and nimbly regained his feet.

Oliver shot him again. In the face. A small round hole appeared in Quist's left cheek, but the wound began to heal, growing visibly smaller in seconds. Behind Oliver, shouts and screams erupted as his assistants began a fierce scramble for the exit.

VAMPIRES OF NIGHTWORLD

David Bischoff

A Del Rey Book

BALLANTINE BOOKS • NEW YORK

A Del Rey Book
Published by Ballantine Books

Copyright © 1981 by David Bischoff

All rights reserved under International and Pan-American
Copyright Conventions. Published in the United States by
Ballantine Books, a division of Random House, Inc., New
York, and simultaneously in Canada by Random House of
Canada, Limited, Toronto, Canada.

Library of Congress Catalog Card Number: 81-65422

ISBN 0-345-28763-0

Manufactured in the United States of America

First Edition: July 1981

Cover art by William Schmidt

For Alan Huff

...nebbishy rain, its nocturnal discharge of light resul-
...dim, until happily whickering hops Charley's valley, but
...assed snow-brine freely through a doubter, blue black
...but they shone only intermittently through the tangle

PROLOGUE

❧━◈━◈━◈━◈━◈━◈❧

'Twas brillig, and the slithy toves
    Did gyre and gimble in the wabe;
All mimsy were the borogoves,
    And the mome raths outgrabe.

—Lewis Carroll

THE JABBERWOCK BURBLED and whiffled through the tulgey wood, a burning fierce in its stomach.

Life was hard for the jabberwock of late. Since Split-Foot had bitten the Big Black and loosed his hold upon the nightcreatures, it was every monster for itself. Now winter sat on its frosted throne and pickings were slim indeed.

The jabberwock gamboled through ermine forest with an odd, wobbling gait, its occasional attempts at flight resulting only in ungainly wing-borne hops. Charon's milky orb strewed moonbeams freely through a cloudless, blue-black sky, but they shone only intermittently through the tangle of skeletal tree limbs that nodded feebly with the winter breeze. The icy ground returned a faerie glitter.

Three-clawed, webbed feet crunched through the friable surface of the snow. Membranous wings were held behind, so as not to impede travel; aloft in bony readiness for brief flight—the only kind of which they were capable. A leathery tail left a sinuous trail in the snow.

The beast was naked save for the crimson waistcoat snug about its brownish-green torso. Coils of mist blossomed wraithlike from a well-fanged mouth, which occupied fully half a sea serpent's face. Baleful eyes bulged below a scaly brow.

If I could manage more stealth, it thought, *I might surprise a deer. How would* that *be, dear friend within. A succulent feast!*

So it approached the wood's edge with as much quiet as possible. The jabberwock slowed and attempted unsuccessfully to conceal its bulk behind a tall, proud oak, naked now of leaves.

Peering into the moon-bright vale, it saw a rabbit. Claws

1

would catch, this eve. Jaws would bite. Rabbit flesh and fur would fill the void within, and then the jabberwock could be about more intellectual business, such as finding employment.

But the rabbit, rather a large one actually, suddenly rose on its strong hind legs. Pink ears cocked back as it reached into its Inverness coat with a paw and fumbled out a gold watch.

"Oh dear! Oh dear! I shall be too late!" it squeaked. Replacing the timepiece, it lowered to all fours and resumed its travel.

The jabberwock was taken aback just long enough for the rabbit to limp, trembling, through the tufts of frozen grass separating it from the forest's edge.

"Bloody Hell!" the jabberwock piped. "Blighter's goin' to be *late* all right if I can help it!" The jabberwock bounded across the vale with haste born of hunger and desperation, then dived into the wood, ignoring the sting of bramble and holly that tore at it, heedless of the din, mindful only of the tidbit bounding away in the darkness. Its nostrils filled with the intoxicating scent of rabbit.

Minutes later, the jabberwock emerged from the forest, puffing but forging valiantly onward, gaining speed as the vegetation thinned.

Before it stood a spired mansion.

Mossy rock walls girded the towers. Cold with a chill beyond mere absence of heat, the castle and its walls seemed composed not of stone and mortar, but chiseled from moonless night skies.

The jabberwock shivered with a dread he'd not felt since commanded by Satan himself. His neck twisted slowly as he scanned the awesome battlements, momentarily forgetting hunger and prey. His immediate inclination was to turn tail and depart, for he preferred to give a wide berth to such places, normally home to creatures more evil than he. He was a pickpocket, a scrounger, a coward, who skulked the day and twilight, skirting the night when he could. There remained, after all, creatures who'd gone quite mad after the Change and, in packs, attacked even noble and innocent jabberwocks.

However, as the jabberwock was about to obey the more reasonable suggestions of his considerable rationality, he caught sight of his intended repast, its fluffy white tail raised with what could only be interpreted as defiance!

The rabbit scampered to the edge of the moat, hopped

onto the lowered drawbridge, and bounded beneath the raised portcullis.

The jabberwock squealed in outrage, then lunged through drifted snow and scampered across the drawbridge. He emerged into a courtyard where walkways had been shoveled clear of snow and hissing torches cast yellowish light over glistening flags. The rabbit was nowhere to be seen.

Dread suddenly overcame the jabberwock, and he turned to flee.

The portcullis slammed home. The torches dimmed, then died out completely.

Whimpering despite himself, the jabberwock turned, eyes vainly searching for another exit, wings flapping slowly.

Something—several somethings?—walked his way.

The jabberwock swiveled and raked his claws against the stout wooden beams of the portcullis. Beyond, a snowfield beckoned in the moonlight.

The jabberwock turned defiantly, hoping to impress whatever surrounded it. "Who's first, then, nightscum? Ain't exactly unprepared, you know!"

A voice replied, one soft, gentle, cultured. "Welcome. And fear not."

A small light was struck, revealing a tall, thin man caped in black. He held the flame in his outstretched, unprotected palm. His eyes were red as backlit rubies.

Standing alongside him, the rabbit smoked a cigar. Its ears flopped about as it bowed in mock deference.

"Please, be our guest," the caped man continued. His gaunt face—with its long, thin nose, high cheekbones, and straight brow—was unmistakable. However, knowledge of his host's identity reassured the jabberwock not at all.

"We have much to talk of, you and I," the man continued. "Of cabbages and kings—" His sudden smile revealed two long needle-thin canines—"and other things."

ACT ONE

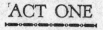

Mark but this flea, and mark in this,
How little that which thou deniest me is;
Me it sucked first, and now sucks thee,
And in this flea our two bloods mingled be.

—John Donne
"The Flea"

vampire's hair was indeed rich black, and its eyes were shiny ... ile out above high, thin cheekbones. The mouth ... particularly long fangs to either side of the row of ...

WHAT AN ODD STATUE, Oliver Dolan thought as he shivered calf-deep in the snow. He had never seen its like. He blew into his mittened hands, which clutched a heavy box.

The killing could wait for a while. Besides, his companions had not finished preparing the bonfire into which the bodies would be tossed.

No doubt about one thing. The subject was a vampire. And no ordinary one at that, from the looks of it.

Remarkable. The monument was of marble with coal black painted on for the cape and cowl, vermilion for the cravat, and white for ruffled cuffs and collar. Pinning the cravat was an ornate insignia in agate and carbuncle. The rings on the pale flesh of its extended fingers were studded with sapphires and rubies. The right hand was open, palming a sphere which supported stylized crimson flames. The vampire's hair was a deep, rich black, and its eyes were afire, peering out above high, thin cheekbones. The mouth sported particularly long fangs to either side of the row of tombstonelike teeth.

A single red icicle, apparently real, hung from the lower left corner of the open mouth.

Oliver Dolan shuddered and took a flask from the pocket of his fur longcoat, then drank the strong brandy; a swallow's worth, no more. Just for warmth.

As the alcohol performed its fleeting dance through his system, he wondered what Geoffrey Turner would have made of this. The statue owned a kind of obscenely self-conscious evil that Oliver had known only in his wildest flights of morbid imagination about Satan's realm. And yet it bespoke a certain intense canniness.

Oliver turned from the statue. The subject was unnerving. Some kind of vampire idol . . . must be. And the bloodsuckers that lived within the crumbling ruins had probably filled its mouth with blood. But why?

Stamping his feet to restore feeling to his legs, Oliver scrutinized the ancient church. Cracked walls held the weather at bay no longer, supported no roof, nor reverberated with prayer. The altar stood naked to the elements. Centuries of exposure had eroded the crucifixes and rusted the metal pulpit. Where pews once stood now lay only winter's pale shroud, a thick mantle of snow as heavy as the fear that weighed Oliver Dolan's heart.

Somewhere below, Oliver thought, *they're sleeping snug and warm, and human blood that is not their own trickles through bodies of flesh, plastic, and steel.*

They had to be destroyed. That lot fell to Oliver.

He despised the chore, not because of its danger, nor because of the atmosphere of evil that pervaded such places as this. He was indifferent to supernatural evil—it simply did not exist for him. No, he hated killing vampires because they were living beings just as much as he, with no choice but to follow the hunger Satan's Prime Directive had programmed in them.

A hand fell on his shoulder.

Startled, he turned and found himself staring into the eyes of his manservant, Caspar Penton.

"You'd best stand by the fire awhile, sir," the man pronounced as best he could through chattering teeth. His large, moist blue eyes avoided the ruins. "The men are about ready. You'll want to warm yourself before we search for the entrance."

"I *want* to be numb, Penton," Oliver whispered. He tucked the lead box beneath the left arm of his fur coat and groped for his flask again. "Numb." As he looked down to locate his pocket, his brown beaver top hat toppled to the snow.

Penton squatted, picked the hat up, brushed it off, and returned it to Oliver with the ceremony only a top-notch gentleman's gentleman can muster. After taking another sip of brandy, Oliver tapped the hat back over his long auburn hair and offered the copper flask to Penton.

"Thank you, sir. Don't mind if I do." He took a long swallow. Licked chapped lips. "Terrible business ahead, sir." Penton screwed the cap back on, then returned the container to its owner, gesturing back with a quick, concise head movement. "Think we have enough men?"

"Ten? Of course that's enough, Penton. With you and me we number twelve, correct? We've done with fewer."

"But we've always known the number of the beasts, and their nature. We're quite far from home on this expedition, sir. Who knows what to expect? I wish you'd taken your father's advice and continued your educational efforts among the emissaries. You endanger yourself too frequently."

8

"I told you," Oliver muttered churlishly, knowing that Penton was quite right, "it was a personal request. The villagers wanted *me* for this task."

"You push yourself too hard, Oliver." Penton pulled the wide lapels of his sheepskin coat up around his thick neck. He flicked snowflakes from the long, waxed mustache beneath his most prominent feature, a round, bulbous nose. "The weight of the world is not to be borne upon your shoulders."

Oliver snorted absently, not really listening. He'd heard the speech too many times. From his father, from his friends. From the asinine ministers. "And I thought this whole episode was finished when Turner and I killed Satan." He rubbed his scarred left arm, then shook his head. "Another time. Another place." He stared at a large van hitched to a pair of roan draft horses. "Suffice it to say that I bought back Turner's van at a most dear price. . . ." His voice trailed off.

"And well you did. But come, sir. The men are waving to us. We must be about our task before the sun sets. This snow has held us up much too long."

Sighing, Oliver allowed himself to be led back to the camp. As he walked, the ruby eyes of the statue seemed to bore into the back of his neck like lasers.

The vampire writhed within a coffin, open to the frigid chapel cellar.

Her hair was a blond medusa of scattered locks. Sweat beaded her pale brow, splotched the underarms of her chemise. The gown's translucence hinted at voluptuousness.

Choked breaths streamed from her clenched teeth. Her bloodshot eyes opened suddenly. Her expression registered terror.

She opened her mouth wide to scream, but a gloved hand quickly stifled the sound into a muffled whimper.

"There, there, sister," a squat, stout man said, holding her firmly. "What is it you see?" His voice was rich with self-confidence. Beneath brown bangs, pinkish eyes burned bright. Carefully, he removed his rough hand.

The woman remained quiet.

"I see," she whispered in a sweet, feminine voice. "I see dark men in the snow, our deaths in their hearts."

The vampire glanced upward fearfully, then turned to the other coffins, closed. Fifteen black coffins, situated in a neat row along the bare, cracked floor. "Thank you, beautiful sentinel. We shall be prepared. Those who threaten shall soon slake our thirst." His face glowed.

Muffled thumping sounded from above.

"Well, where d'ya think it is then, eh?" the wide, swarthy man growled. His large right hand clutched a hammer and a stake. Though he spoke with bluff casualness, his eyes betrayed his true emotions; they darted about fearfully. "I don't see no way down inside. I say just forget it. Wait till spring thaw."

Assenting mutters greeted his words.

Oliver Dolan turned wearily toward them. "Very well. But I'll not be here. Nor my weapons. I'll do my best to instruct you when we return to your village." He began to trudge back through the snow, Caspar Penton on his heels.

"Wait a bleedin' moment for the love of God." The swarthy man stepped forward to grasp Oliver's passing arm. "*You* won't have to live here in these parts, sleep nights afraid you might wake up with your throat torn out."

Oliver thrust the man's arm away. "Very well. Shall we proceed? I assure you, I've little taste for this task. I shall turn back at the least complaint about my leadership." He swung his head, regarding the others resolutely. "Is that understood?"

Mumbles of grudging assent were voiced.

"Let's get on with it, then."

Through the driving snow, Oliver walked to the altar at the chapel's rear. The cold pierced him mercilessly, from within, from without. In one hand he carried a six-barreled pistol, in the other the box. They were part of the legacy of Geoffrey Turner and his wondrous van. Within the box lay a cross whose rays, though merely painful to human flesh for short periods, interfered somehow with the internal machinery of the vampires. His own cross, a gift from Turner, had saved Oliver's life many times.

"Now," he continued. "Before we find the entrance, shall I answer any more questions?"

"Yessir." A tall man stepped forward. He held a double-barreled shotgun. "You sure these things are going to kill the bastards?"

Oliver gazed upward, as if for help. But his eyes met only the low-slung clouds, gray and indifferent. "How often must I repeat myself? The vampires, the entire menagerie of Styxian beasts of what we called Nightworld, are *not* supernatural. They are creatures of flesh and steel—different from us, most assuredly, but nonetheless obeying physical laws, the same under which we operate. They are quite vulnerable to common weapons, albeit hard to kill. But the crosses—their *radiations* actually—will hold powerful creatures at bay until we can hammer our explosive stakes in, blow their mechanical brains out, or whatever. Have I made myself clear?"

"I should think," Penton added, "that Mr. Dolan knows that of which he speaks."

"An' when they're dead why not just straightforward chuck 'em in the fire?"

Oliver sighed. "The fire is to satisfy *your* needs; *I'd* like to gut the creatures of their mechanisms. I have knowledge of their function. Some parts may well be of use one day, when we come to understand them fully. Besides, metal, plastic, and glass are most valuable."

"You do what you like," one of them grumbled, a well-muscled lad whose fat cheeks were red with the cold. "But let's kill the things first."

"Good idea!" Oliver smiled wryly. He turned and began to search for an entrance. "Normally, a door, I'd say, somewhere in the walls." He eyed the ruined walls. "Here, perhaps, a trapdoor. With a ring on it—confounded snow covers everything."

Seeing no door, the men scuffed their feet about, searching for the posited trapdoor.

Suddenly, Caspar Penton stumbled. "I believe I've found it, sir."

Heavy boots made speedy work of the snow. Beneath, around the thick brass ring that Oliver had predicted, crystals of blood clung to stone, spoor of the creatures who had passed that way by night. Although the vampires and the other minions of Satan could now walk the day if they chose, most still preferred the concealment of night for their activity, preying not merely on the blood of normal folk, but the fear, a residue of five centuries of horror. In the eighteen months since Oliver had walked, seemingly victorious, from Computer Mountain, only a fraction of the world had learned the true facts relating to the situation of Styx. The others—well, the others knew that things had changed somewhat, but had no idea why. In dark moments, Oliver felt that by killing Satan and freeing His Creatures, he and Turner had only confused matters. If anything, Nightworld had become more deadly, because it was less predictable.

Independent of the programmed constraints of Hedley Nicholas, the cyborg psychotic who thought himself Lucifer, Scourge of God Incarnate, most of the nightcreatures were now free-lance rogues, scrounging for food and power, developing minds of their own, and integrating themselves into human society.

Night no longer was their prison. Day no longer promised safety from their attack.

Swallowing his fear, Oliver knelt by the stone trapdoor. "A knife!" he called. A wood-handled blade was pressed into his open palm, and he chopped at the ice that glued handle to pocked stone. Soon, the ring was free, the door uncovered. Oliver gripped the ring and tugged upward, straining. The thick slab moved only an inch. Oliver let go and it fell into place with a muffled thump. He stood and brushed his hands absently. "Strong buggers. One of them alone can lift that." He sighed. "Well. Nothing for it. Rope, please."

A coil of hemp was provided. Tying one end tightly around the gray-green brass ring, Oliver tossed the rest over the eight-foot wall beside him. "Makeshift pulley, you know," he explained, pointing. "Snow and ice should protect the rope as it rubs against the edge. Four of you"—he quickly tapped the brawniest for the task—"get on the other side. Pull. Then tie the rope securely about something and return. I want us all together as we begin the descent." The four scrambled over the ruined wall.

The rope grew taut, and the trapdoor grated open slowly, until it stood perpendicular to the floor.

"Right," Oliver whispered. "Quiet as possible, now! They'll be sleeping. Surprise will help. I'm going to drop in. Doesn't look deep. Use the other rope if you like. We'll need it to climb out, anyway. But I'd appreciate a rapid entry from you all before they rouse. Penton and I will descend first—got your stuff, old man?"

Betraying no emotion, Penton patted his own lead box.

"Right ho. Torches, please." Two were offered. Their oily stench offended Oliver, but the extra light reassured him. "Follow us as quickly as possible. And be prepared for the fight of your lives."

Squatting, Oliver thrust the torch into the black maw of the cellar. He could make out the floor, perhaps eight feet below.

"Perhaps, sir," Penton said, "a hand down would be in order."

Oliver shook his head, and in one fluid motion slipped over the side into the chamber.

He landed on both feet. Torchlight revealed a large chamber filled with a musky fetidness. But the sharp, coppery undertaste of blood was unmistakable. But where was the electric tingle to which Oliver had become so accustomed in nightcreature lairs? Where the hum and hiss of recharging machinery? No lights ablink here. No reddish mounds glowed.

Oliver took a tentative step forward, as much to remove himself from the path of Penton's leap as to explore. His torchlight forged ahead, revealing nothing but bare stone. He drew his electric torch from his pocket, snapped it on. Its strong beam leaped to the far side of the room and revealed rows of closed coffins.

Another torch flared downward and Penton followed immediately, landed improperly, and toppled to his buttocks with an angry "Ooooff!" Oliver helped him to his feet.

"You all right, old man?"

"Yes, yes, just my dignity scathed, I think. I do wish, though, we'd used the rope to climb down here. Bit of a jump."

"I prefer a speedy and abrupt entrance, as well you know; the rope is reserved for our exit." He retrieved Penton's torch and handed it to him, then shone his flashlight toward the coffins. "All at rest, I think," he whispered. "But I must admit, there is something most odd."

"Odd, sir?"

"Look about you. No machinery. The *smell* is right. Vampires are here, no doubt about that. But where is their equipment?"

"Hard to say, sir. Perhaps we should retreat. Abnormality portends difficulty."

"No. No, if things are different I must find out why. Here, let's secure our torches. Darkness is their ally, not ours."

Quickly, they located sconces and inserted their torches. Two more of the townsfolk of Perth had joined them, wide-eyed and tense with caution.

"Let's have a look at these coffins, Penton," Oliver said, taking a torch from a new arrival. "Crosses at ready!"

"Should we not wait for the others? Safety in numbers, after all." A mild tremor had crept into Penton's voice.

Oliver stared back at the man. Caspar Penton had been in his service for some ten months. Viscount Dolan, Oliver's father, had thought it appropriate that his bachelor son should be attended properly, and therefore acquired a gentleman's gentleman for the twenty-one-year-old.

Oliver had gone through three before he'd hit upon Penton. Two departed the day after their hiring, immediately upon learning of Oliver Dolan's peculiar employment. The other lasted two weeks, dying beneath the claws of a particularly nasty gryphon Oliver had thought to exterminate. Suddenly, help became very hard to procure. But then, seemingly from nowhere, the fortyish, balding Penton—mustache, placid blue eyes and all—had arrived on horseback in search of employment. Penniless, desperate he'd been then. How those eyes had lit to learn that yes, Viscount Dolan's heir would be happy of his service at a goodly three hundred and twenty pounds *per annum*. A quick physical and comprehensive testing in proficiency with firearms and swords ("Started out with m'Lord Shrafter's regiment, don't you know, way off 'cross the Straits. And you ask if I can handle a pistol!") had shown the stranger fit and worthy in Oliver's eyes.

A detailed recitation of all that would be expected of Oliver Dolan's manservant had not deterred the man, although Oliver thought he had noted a brief expression of chagrin crossing the man's face when he thought he was not being observed.

Obviously, the fellow needed money. Obviously, he cared not at all how he was called upon to serve. But he was damned good. And, generally, Oliver listened to any voicing of trepidation on his part. However, Oliver was now intent upon the eradication of this nest of vampires, and, most particularly, the discovery of cause for the *strangeness* he felt in the den.

Oliver waved away the manservant's doubts. "I've dealt with more than these, alone, as well you know. The crosses will protect us no matter how many pop up, Penton. Come on. We'll get stinking drunk afterward in celebration." Oliver drew his lead box from beneath his arm, lifted the hasp, and marched forward.

With a helpless sigh, Penton followed, his own box at the ready.

Behind them, the others—steadily increasing in number as men clumsily fell to the cellar floor—hung back, waiting for the more venturesome strangers to test the unknown.

Had Oliver deigned to peer over his shoulder, he would have seen the rope being prepared for the speedy exit of these, the bravest folk of Perth.

A quick count showed fifteen coffins. Not unusual. The blood stench grew as he approached the coffins. A prolonged creak broke the quiet, and a slick mahogany coffin lid rose steadily. Oliver could easily discern the pale-skinned hand that lifted the lid with long, tapered fingers. Suddenly, dark and graceful, a figure lifted itself nimbly from the oblong box and stepped out. Its shiny black leather pumps clacked on stone. The creature stood erect and proud before them, a man wearing a modestly cut tweed morning suit, predominantly gray. Soft brown curls spilled over small ears and an unprepossessing forehead. His features were delicate and well formed with not a hint of the deadly ferocity Oliver had learned to associate with the bloodsucker's ilk. Thin lips broke into a hesitant smile. All in all, he seemed more like a customs house clerk on holiday than a warm-blooded killer.

"Good day," he said in a small, whispery voice. "May I help you?"

He clasped his hands before a wide checked tie which disappeared into a thick brown cardigan.

Oliver was momentarily speechless, but his resolute intent won over his shock at the meekness of this particular specimen of nightcreature. They were certainly more eccentric nowadays.

"Yes," he said, stepping forward, chin high as he opened the lid toward the man. A glow sprung from the radioactive material within. It bathed the man's mild face in unearthly radiance. "You can be quick about dying."

"What a *nice* cross! Day-glo?"

"You're—you're not a vampire?" The words escaped in a sort of gasp. In Oliver's experience, vampires routinely cringed and backed away from the radioactive bath. "Then what are you doing here, in that box?"

"Well, of *course* I'm a vampire!" His nostrils flared. "Is there something wrong with that?" He sniffed. His thin, sensitive hands fluttered like small birds contending for a favorite perch. Then his eyelids lowered.

"Did you say you wanted me to . . . die?" His voice was troubled.

The previous sense of authority that had nerved Oliver for the task, the dutiful righteousness that had buoyed him through months of fierce combat with Satan's creatures, abruptly disappeared. "Um, well, yes—of course! But you can't be a vampire. This cross doesn't affect you."

The vampire shrugged. "Times have changed, dear boy. Tell me—just how long have you experienced the desire to destroy vampires? Has it anything to do with . . . certain frustrated drives?" He arched his eyebrows coyly.

"What?" Oliver was incredulous. He recovered his resolve immediately. "Listen, good fellow. If you're a vampire, you drink human blood—correct?"

"Absolutely." He bared a canine. "Delicious stuff. But you, sir, *eat* flesh, do you not?" The man scowled in disgust. *"That* is barbarous!"

Oliver blinked in vexation. "But I mean, you killed five people!" He made an abrupt, directionless gesture. "I mean, five people from Perth are *missing,* and their trails lead here. That's why I was asked in."

"And who, pray tell, are *you?"*

"I'm—Oliver Dolan. Geoffrey Turner and I killed Satan in his stronghold a year and a half ago."

The vampire's eyebrows raised. "Oh, *really?"* The creature quickly strode forward and shook Oliver's hand before the young man could react. The vampire's palm was cold and somewhat clammy. One pump and the creature resumed its previous distance. "Such an honor to *meet* you, sir! We've heard much about you. You're the one that started things, you know. Absolutely! I understand that things were so terribly *dismal* for nightfolk before you and the mandroid lush lumbered your way to Hell and offed old Brimstone Breath. Good job, chappie. We'll be so glad to have you among us."

" 'Among us'?" Penton echoed, stepping back a pace while raising his pistol slightly. "What do you mean by that?"

"Well, you admit you are here to destroy my companions and myself, do you not?" The creature raised his arms in an expansive gesture. "You, and those fellows climbing that rope there."

Oliver spun about and screeched: "Cowards! Stay! We'll need you all!" One man was already halfway through the trapdoor. The others hovered anxiously below. Stakes, hammers, and cross boxes lay scattered about; drawn pistols quivered in the murky torchlight.

"Don't like it!" said one of the men. "Not at all. 'Taint what you'd said it'd be like."

"You needn't bother yourselves," the vampire said, examining a fingernail nonchalantly. "You won't escape." He looked up mildly; but the sharp fangs that showed in his mouth belied the harmless expression. He gazed around at the deeper shadows. "But then why should they want to, eh, Harold?"

From a point to the rear of the chamber, where the meager torchlight did not reach, a small child of perhaps five years emerged, a boy, foppishly dressed in brown velvet shorts and jacket, golden curls streaming about a rosy-cheeked face.

"Sweet God," one of the men cried behind Oliver. "It's my Harold!" Long scarf trailing on the floor, the man ran toward the new arrival, who had stopped beside the vampire. The little boy's eyes shone.

Oliver grabbed at the man's arm, halting him. "Renbard—no, man! I don't know what's happening, but it's not—"

The little boy spoke, extending his arms in childish exuberance. "Oh, Father! Father! Come and play with Mr. Quist and me." His freckled snub nose twitched disarmingly. "It's so lovely here with my friends. It's ever so grand, Father!"

Renbard tore from Oliver's grasp and stumbled to his son, arms outstretched. He stooped to enfold the child in a warm, paternal hug. The boy, with an expression of unalloyed glee, snuggled his cute face into the juncture of neck and shoulder, little arms draped around his father's back.

Beaming, Mr. Quist looked down on the reunion like a fond uncle.

"Oliver," Penton whispered. "We're not prepared for this. I suggest we sound retreat, what?"

Suddenly, with a muffled choke, Renbard stiffened. The little boy's tousled blond head was bobbing slowly up and down. A snuffling sound emanated from the pair. Then the father relaxed, his weight breaking the boy's grasp. He tumbled to the cold flags, eyes staring up at the dim ceiling. Two crimson welts oozed blood.

Harold, betraying two long fangs through a cherubic smile, smacked his lips and clapped his hands in a spontaneous expression of joy. Bright streams of red clung to his chin. He flicked at them with a finger, licked at it as a child might a lollipop, then bent over his father's neck for more.

Mr. Quist looked up at his visitors, obviously quite

17

pleased. "Isn't that sweet? Always touching to see a father care for his son." Mr. Quist chuckled deep in his throat, a sound of honest amusement.

The chuckle nudged Oliver from his reverie of horror. He snapped the case shut and raised the revolver he carried.

Mr. Quist slowly held out his hand. "Now, now. That won't do you any good at all, sir. Please. I believe young Harold was—"

With a roar, Oliver stepped forward and shoved the boy from his father. Surprised by the attack, Harold was flung to the ground. His face mirrored his disorientation briefly, then dissolved into tears.

Oliver swung to face Mr. Quist, who was frowning.

"That was quite uncalled for. However, we will give you the benefit of the doubt. In the meantime, a spokesman."

Another vampire stepped from the darkness. Attired in hunting tweeds, he wore a dark mauve deerstalker cap above his thickset, ruddy face.

Behind Oliver a voice sounded, identifying the man. "That's Bill Thorndyke, the gamekeeper. 'E's another one of the missin'. What's wrong with his eyes, for the love of God?"

Thorndyke's eyes were red-rimmed, red-pupiled; his expression smoldered with almost religious fervor. It was as if the eyes were aflame and his unruly hair the smoke.

"We have before us those who balk at joining our number," Mr. Quist said. "Lend a few encouraging words for their benefit."

A blissful smile lit the vampire's face. "Once, I lived as an animal, seeking what I craved in alehouse cups. I groveled in my world much as a pig grovels in its sty, and knew not the Way until I was blessed by the Blood Kiss, the Life Kiss, and I just pray to Our Father that my mouth will taste the ecstasy of our guests' passing into our ways."

"Now, sirs. Does that sound so very bad? So, if you just remain very still—" Mr. Quist smiled, raised a finger, crooked it—"until we can visit you with our Joy most peacefully."

From the shadows the rest of their number emerged. They must have known of the killing party's arrival!

Twelve more: men, women, children with an ecstatic hunger in their eyes. They did not shuffle, but walked quite normally. Their eyes betrayed them, though, as did the hint of old blood that wafted before them. Otherwise, they seemed perfectly normal; people you might pass in the street.

"We must deal with them, men——" Oliver aimed his pistol—"as best we can!"

He squeezed the trigger. Flame spat from the barrel. In such close quarters, the report was overwhelming.

Taken full in the chest with the bullet, Mr. Quist toppled backward, then pushed his coffin onto the floor. But the self-satisfied smile never left his face.

He lay quietly upon the floor for a few seconds, then drew one large breath and regained his feet.

Oliver shot him again, full in the face.

The entry wound was clear; a small round hole in the left cheek. Mr. Quist's head jerked back, never losing its smile. A drop of blood dribbled down the side of the face— a curiously purple shade of red, not like normal human blood.

Before Oliver's eyes, the wound began to heal, growing visibly smaller in seconds.

Shouts and screams erupted as a fierce scramble for the rope began.

The vampires surged forward, ready to visit their communion upon the disorganized humans before them.

"No, you idiots!" Oliver cried as he and Penton gave ground before the slow advance of the attackers. "The stakes! The stakes *must* work!"

But the explosive devices lay, forgotten, on the floor as the townsfolk fought among themselves for first access to the rope. Only one man—a nimble fellow who had been entrusted with the electric bident—maintained his presence of mind. He dashed forward, weapon at the ready, the battery cannister power cable flapping. He rushed past Oliver, face alive with fury.

"No, Curtis!" Oliver shouted above the din. "If the cross has no effect on them, there can be no internal machinery for you to short out!"

Oblivious, the young fellow dove into the pack of vampires. He took the first—a fat character in peasant clothing—directly in the abdomen, just as Oliver had so patiently instructed. Immediately, one hand streaked to the black cannister strapped to his chest and flicked on the power switch.

Electricity crackled. The fat man began to burn, but he betrayed no pain. With a single heave, he pushed his attacker away and ripped the spear from his own belly with

19

a pronounced *thuck*. He fell upon the stunned young man, mouth wide, ready to sink long teeth.

Oliver searched about desperately. He saw a fallen stake, with a hammer beside it. Quickly he waded through the melee and scooped up the weapons. The creatures could not be completely impervious to physical force, though they were obviously quite powerful. Bullet, spear, club, or knife would not do. Nothing short of an explosive would be effective. The only weapons of that nature on hand were the scattered stakes.

Oliver grabbed at the stake and hammer, then spun around.

The scruffy fellow who had so quickly dispatched young Curtis turned his attention upon Oliver, stepping directly toward him. Oliver took a firm grip on the stake and rushed forward, burying the tempered tip six inches below his ribs. Purplish blood welled.

Oliver pressed the detonating stud. He heard a muffled thump. Immediately the creature's chest and back blew out, scattering flesh and bone in a wide arc. The vampire, blood gushing from its mouth, staggered backward. It stared at Oliver, disbelief and pain etched on its face. Then the red eyes filmed, and the legs gave way. A cloud of sulfurous smoke hung where the beast had stood.

Astonished vampire eyes turned upon Oliver.

Oliver tossed the charred remains of the stake at the nearest men and yelled, "Use the stakes! Go to the van! More stakes! And acid!" Oliver cast about for another weapon. They'd brought plenty—if only the stupid peasants had not dropped them!

Even as he stooped to pick up another stake, the vampires renewed their attack. Though the creatures were not as strong as the cyborg vampires that Oliver had encountered earlier, Oliver and his companions were outnumbered. That some of the attackers were women and children did not seem to decrease the effectiveness of the onslaught, for the fangs of the lesser vampires were as sharp, and their movements more lithe. There would be no escape short of victory.

Bodies rolled, fangs flashed in the guttering torchlight, blood dripped from wounds on both sides. Havoc reigned for confused moments, and still shots rang out, useless.

Two vampires, rightly distinguishing him as the greatest danger, closed on Oliver. One was a teenaged boy, perhaps three years younger than Oliver, the other a beautiful woman with auburn hair.

Hesitating only a moment, Oliver thrust at her torso, thumb over the firing stud of the stake. The woman dodged, then leaped to his side, burying fingernails in his shoulders, through his greatcoat. He tried to shake her off, but the woman clung tenaciously. Her cold breath was foul.

Immediately the younger vampire jumped, mouth agape, but Oliver shoved his weapon's narrow end into its throat. Before the gurgling creature could pull away, Oliver thumbed the stud, causing a momentary bloody rain over the thrashing din. Immediately, another muffled explosion erupted, and, turning, Oliver saw the tattered figure of Penton rise above the lifeless body of a vampire.

A maddened scream seized Oliver's attention as the female vampire leaped upon him, straddling him, bearing him down to the damp floor with her shrill fury. The clawed hands released his shoulders to tear at his face. Oliver caught them by the wrists, and the vampire woman growled with frustration. Then icy red lips curled back as her head made a dive for his jugular. He struck out at her face, but succeeded only in nicking his hand on her canines.

Nearer and nearer the perfumed mouth drifted, a slow-motion dream of rapturous death that whispered with more excitement than life ever owned. Oliver tried to scramble to his feet, but seemed weakened somehow. The auburn hair seemed to undulate like a gorgon's snakes, writhing silently in their deadly dance. Finally, Oliver could see only the teeth, the glistening fangs descending toward his unprotected throat.

A blaze of pure white flashed into view. A meteor streak, it seemed. Briefly, Oliver caught sight of a floppy felt hat, a long fluffy scarf stirring with the liquid movement of its owner, who was swinging a long rapier.

Snicker snack!

The rapier flicked with precision, burned through the air, bit through the back of the vampire's neck, slashing straight through to the other side. Eyes frigidly glazed, mouth an O of surprise, the head toppled forward. Arterial blood geysered from the body, which tottered but a moment before it sprawled backward.

The roar of the conflict ceased.

Oliver blinked. All eyes in the room were directed at the apparition.

21

The man stood tall and whip-thin, a stiff black cloth coat belling from a tight leather belt about his midsection. The brass buttons of his coat rode a muscular chest, up to the broad lapels. Amused green eyes gleamed from a face like the sharp end of a hatchet: hawk-nose, small, pursed mouth, jutting chin. Long-fingered, delicate hands framed by crisp white cuffs grasped the hilt of a rapier, four feet of burning blade.

The man bowed curtly, briefly disturbing well-groomed brown hair that curled from beneath a wide-brimmed hat. The air about him was filled with an electric charge, smelling of the wind advancing before a thundershower.

"Who *are* you?" Oliver asked, his voice betraying his astonishment.

"My name," the man said with a faint Scottish burr, "is Roald MacPherson. I am an Angel of the Lord, at the service of God—and, at present, yourself." He whipped the sword about. It left an after-image in the dark. "Now, we have a few more demons to destroy, I think."

With a grim smile framing even white teeth, he advanced into the fray.

"MELODRAMA, MY DEAR JABBERWOCK. Melodrama and genetic engineering. Flesh and blood are putty to my fingers; steel and wiring, sculptures of my mind. I am the play director and the puppeteer. *Artiste* and artist—the palette my nightcreatures, Styx my canvas. But I shall add *color* to the shades of black and white *my* creator constructed. And music!"

A finger tap-danced on a bank of buttons and toggles. Soft music twinkled from speakers, harpsichord Bach. Vlad Paler cocked an ear and shut his eyes, relishing the sound. "Yes, the drama of my life—my world—shall have music. The characters will loom large and deceptively simple, for symbols needs must tread archetypal pathways, teeter on stereotype to weave the complex pattern. A game and yet much more." He blinked, then focused across the length of the desk. "I say, Jabberwock, would you care to do some drugs?"

In his present state, semiconsciousness, the jabberwock could only gurgle and drool. He sat, bound by heavy chains and rope, against the wall of a chamber filled with the bric-a-brac of an Earth long dead. The jabberwock's first thought was for Hampton, and he was vaguely comforted by an awareness of the presence in its belly chamber. *Fear not, Hampton, for death alone can separate us,* the jabberwock thought. *Here, always here, pal,* Hampton responded.

"But of course! Now, if I can just find my syringe. We have cocaine, heroin, lysergic acid, morsia, gefto, and all kinds of substances I have synthesized for my amusement. Taken in conjunction with the appropriate electrical stimuli, they are especially appropriate for cyborgs like you or myself." Vlad smiled and extracted a leather case from between two yellowing volumes. "But for this little talk, I think we shall stick to simple cocaine and a bracing cup of tea."

The jabberwock managed to croak, "Just tea, thank you."

"Very well. It appears I've only one needle, anyway. And I'd have to visit the lab for a syringe with sufficient capacity for one such as yourself. Milk and sugar?"

The jabberwock blinked.

"In your tea."

"Oh. Right."

Paler stroked a button and spoke into an intercom. "Two cups of Earl Grey, scullery. One eight-ounce and one half-a-gallon. And several tins of biscuits, cream-filled." The vampire looked up at the jabberwock. "Crumpets?"

The jabberwock nodded as his vision finally cleared. He shuddered. Things weren't at all as he'd expected when the vampires had swarmed over him with clubs and chloroform—dungeons and spiders and straw, yes; not a cheerful fire, baroque music, and tea. Somehow, the unexpected bonhomie was spookier than the darkness.

Automatically, his bulging eyes began to assay the room's trappings, but fear speedily overcame greed and larcenous thoughts disappeared.

"Five dozen crumpets. Fresh, Scrazz—not yesterday's, mind!" A deep voice affirmed the order, and Vlad rubbed his hands delightedly. "Now, where was I, Jabberwock?"

Almost recovered, the jabberwock vainly attempted to rise. "You said something about melodrama. What in God's name is going on here?" The creature's wings, his only free appendages, flapped woefully.

"My, my. A bit tetchy now, are we? But let us pretend to a civility we do not own—let us be gentlevampire and gentlecreature. Patience, Jabberwock." The vampire's deft hands were attending all the while to syringe and vial and candle. "Explanations will come."

"Listen, mate, you've got the wrong nightcreature. I've no tiff with you, nor you with me. Let's just have our tea and I'll disregard the kidnapping and not have my several hundred friends rip you to shreds."

The vampire removed his jacket and rolled up the silk sleeve of his shirt. "What a fine actor you'll be. Fire and flair and gusto! That's why you jabberwocks are so much more interesting than dragons. That's one of the reasons I want your help. Just one."

The needle penetrated the pale flesh above the left elbow.

The vampire relaxed somewhat. He sat lightly in his high-backed chair, eyes half open. The creature had a certain Byronic flair, he moved with animation and grace, and yet there was an aura about him that suggested he was merely a talented actor, juggling a trunk's worth of masks. Handsome, he had about the body and face the appearance of youth and vitality. But in his eyes were hints of darkness, of a sadness that his spritely actions would not acknowledge.

And in his mouth, of course, were his teeth.

"Melodrama," the vampire repeated. He swung his arms theatrically. "Thrills and laughter and panache and pathos in three action-filled acts. Jabberwock, I want to make you a star, a part of delicious evil, frightful frivolity, and ultimate victory. I'll pay for your services, you incredibly ugly beast, and you shall rank high when the new order takes its place on this most delightful planet!"

"I don't want anything to do with you, mate. I'm a thief and a rotter, but I'll not link up with no vampires. I didn't like your sort when old Nick was calling the shots."

"No," the man murmured. "No one much did, did they?"

"Who are you?"

"Me? Of course! I've been so excited, I've neglected proper introductions."

The vampire stood, and walked to the scrolled mantelpiece above the wavering fire. He stared at his reflection in the mirror. "You know, Jabberwock—"

"Darkwing," the jabberwock said.

"How poetic, dear product of poetry. And I? I am the product of legend, of what the mass unconscious saw lurking in the night, not realizing that the night was innocent—the evil lurked in themselves. Darkwing, vampires do not reflect in the mirror according to the tales in my library. Yet I see mine. I'll tell you why—I, like you, am a creation of Hedley Nicholas, madman *nonpareil*. Deluded Satan of Nightworld. I presume you know something of our late master's background."

"This and that."

"And it doesn't matter a jot, so long as your belly's full, does it? What a wonderful world this is, Darkwing." He raised his head toward the ceiling and laughed. "A warped mirror of literary and legendary reality. Fairy tales turned head over heels. Why, it's the externalized mass subconscious posited by Carl Jung. Properly controlled, Styx can be a living monument to imagination. And it's *my* playground now, not that of the late, lamented, and demented Lucifer."

"You're bloody mad, mate."

"I'm a bit of a God, you know, Darkwing." He raised his hands defensively. "Now don't get me wrong. I'm no madder than any artist, and I'm certainly not a Caligula or even a Hedley Nicholas—I've no delusions of grandeur.

25

No, my illusions I recognize as such—and intend to render in bold reality!"

Vlad was interrupted by the advent of several servants bearing trays. Tea was served by an attractive young woman in a short dress who stood quietly alongside the jabberwock, popping crumpets and biscuits into his maw and offering up slurps of tea from an ice bucket at what seemed appropriate times. Feet propped atop his ornate walnut desk, Vlad held a china cup daintily in one hand, its saucer in the other, and continued his exposition.

"I was one of Hedley Nicholas's early experiments. I think old Nick was getting a trifle lonely about then. Needed a right-hand man! So he added just a bit more intelligence to one of his vampires, and *voilà*. Me, Vlad M. Paler—no, no, the name was my choice. Had a number and that was all, according to Satan, just as we all did.

"Wretched fellow. Oh, I sucked up to him like a child to ice cream. Your Majesty, Your Greatness gleams like the stars in a night sky." Vlad turned and addressed an imaginary Satan above him. "Your Malevolence, I worship you as any creature adores life. Of course, Father of Evil, I am perfecting the processes You desire—genetics, chromosomes for evil, disease vectors, DNA warriors. Soon, under Your leadership, Styx will be in Your grasp. The plague of vampirism will spread like sand upon the wind's breath, and all true humans will call *You* master. Oh, *how* I long for the moment, great Lucifer."

Vlad Paler shrugged lightly, then sipped his tea. "Utterly ridiculous, groveling before a lunatic who commanded more power than he used—and owned less power than he thought." He closed his eyes and murmured to himself. Bangs curled over his forehead, lending him an air of Keatsian melancholy. The jabberwock had only half listened to the vampire's ranting while feverishly casting about for some method of escape.

Suddenly, Vlad's eyes sprang open, incredibly wide. His voice was a croaking whisper. "And all the while I plotted. I drank my blood like a good little vampire, and my will grew strong. Soon, my power reached through Satan's ranks, through peoples of Styx, until I had laboratories, genetic vats, computers, all created from spares Satan permitted me. He never understood the stuff that composed his machine self, never—and I did. My genius grew and so did my power. If I had had one year more, one year!—" the vampire's hand snatched at empty air—"this world would have been mine, and my philosophies would have ended its stupidities—and its prime clown, Satan himself."

"What happened?"

Vlad bounced to his feet. "Oh, just a woman. I thought she had me by the neck, but she had me by the heart. She was the joy of my existence, and the end of my ambitions, for, once, after a tiff, she muttered a few words within earshot of Old Nick's prime flunky—and *puff!* Rebellion died stillborn and its vampire minions were exterminated."

"And what became of you?"

"Destruction was too good for me!" Paler's voice became a barely controlled snarl. "I still had my uses. In my own castle, I was placed in suspended animation. Cold, cold, so very cold it was, and my brain was violated by their wires, my consciousness numbed, my intelligence tapped for the memory nodes of a computer. Half of the more imaginative beasties that prowl this planet are the stuff of my imagination. And I? I was in the center of Hell, packed in ice. Dantean, don't you think? Steely Satan an unwitting master of irony. And there I rotted, half alive, for centuries."

The servants bowed their heads in sympathy. The jabberwock bent his limber neck toward the woman with the bucket of tea and did his best at a whisper: "Let me go and I'll get you out of this, dear lady."

The woman did not move, staring entranced at her master.

"Bloody Hell," the jabberwock murmured.

A thin, sharp fingernail reared in the air. "And then, a year and a half ago, I was freed. Satan was dead. Control over me—and his nightcreatures—was relaxed. I had my castle again; I had my life again; and joy of joys, I had my dreams again."

"Yes," Darkwing said. "But the story has puzzled me because it always mentions that Satan was defeated by a mandroid from the legendary lands where Satan himself was born."

"Yes, yes! Chap named Geoffrey Turner. Mandroid manufactured by Queen Victoria herself after the fabric of the early H. G. Wells. After the Empire crumbled Nicholas welded himself into the computer, and Turner tried for five centuries to stop the lunacy. The result? Why, the world we have now. It is the stuff of absurdity, our present reality, but it *is* real. It is ours, and we must bend it to our own inner truths. Don't you see?" His eyes

27

fired with manic glee. "We have all mythology and more to work with, to fashion a truly marvelous world of dark and shadow, of bright jewels and fair ladies, of imagination gone gaga." He pointed to a batch of papers. "Just as I write plays, so will I write the history of this world, and it shall be a work of art." He shuffled through the pile. "At the moment, I'm beginning a history of all that is to happen in the next few months, and this will be of prime importance—prime importance!" He smiled with great enthusiasm. "Shall I read you some of it?"

"Couldn't we skip to my part?"

The vampire pouted. "You wanted to know what happened to rid this world of Satan, didn't you? Well, this part tells you. Part of my prologue."

"I suppose I don't have much choice."

"No. You don't." Vlad cleared his throat loudly. "All right, we'll start with a chap named Oliver Dolan. Now remember, this might not be *entirely* true, but then that's what poetry's all about. Right."

Vlad raised his hand melodramatically, and began solemnly to intone the verse.

"And from the sky there dropped a metal star,
A forged life form by otherwheres infested,
The cream of Eden hunting curdled milk.
Fresh-stocked with fires of the Sun, they held
The weapons of the morn, mounted refulgent,
The bane of magic, sorcery's analogue.
They breathed their threatening vapors into Hell,
Where Satan writhed upon his wires. Full-vexed,
He hexed their coming with his creatures' might.
Dragon-fire tongues tasted the ship's corona
And beasts of lowest mind-depth railed and clawed
And pounced with fury of electric spell;
Yet entry was not gained, nor entity
Disgorged before infernal eyes. A comet
New to Heaven had announced the ship
Before its advent, and the hordes of HOPE,
Their passions burning for the remembered Queen,
Sought now to tumble Satan from his throne.
Bold Geoffrey, holder of capon and cup,
Across the breadth of Fernwold did traverse,
There to enlist within his quest a youth,
One *Oliver* of *Dolan*. All their tales
Are ten-times sung, of werewolves, wurdalaks

And worms thrice conquered. In the final fray,
With woman from another world allied,
Razors of light their swords, they braved perdition
To split the life of Split-Foot from the world's
Mechanic bowel. Geoffrey's fleshy form
He left behind; the woman from the planet
Soon was gone; young Oliver alone
Returned to heal his wounded land and soul.
But Satan's headless tentacles, alight
With their own fires, came new to life beneath
The rocks of night. To claim their own they fought
And rallied new toward a Promised One."

The jabberwock, discomfort overcoming his dread, interrupted sarcastically. *"Who* might the Promised One be?"

Vlad bowed modestly. He tossed his composition back to
the desk. "I mentioned the youth. Oliver Dolan." His voice
was strained. "Although I owe him much, he has become
an unwelcome antagonist in my tale. His innocent exuberance has become fanaticism; his life's work appears
to be the eradication of nightcreatures. Can it be long before he detects the flow of my lovely virus and directs his
campaign against my companions and myself? Even as we
speak, he has found a den of my children. And there is
aught I can do to assist them. I need a very special opera-
tive. A servant of guile and cunning, discreet yet with the
strength and wit necessary to destroy this Dolan or persuade
him to visit me here at my castle. Alone. I am well ac-
quainted with jabberwocks, friend Darkwing. For I designed your breed and all its idiosyncrasies during my
service to Satan. You are my child, Jabberwock. And your
father asks only a tiny favor, one for which he will reward
you richly."

Life had taught the jabberwock that when he could not
bully he should grovel, and a life's practice caused an
automatic response even as he sought internal comfort
from Hampton. "Of course, guv'nor. Absolutely and un-
questionably. Point me to the scruffy assassin and claws
will catch, jaws will bite. I shall dedicate myself to your
service!" *We get out of here, Hampton, and we run the
opposite way. You'll be safe, luv.*

Vlad stroked his cheek slowly. "How sweet. But you
haven't much choice, Jabber darling. I will insure your
loyalty in several ways. And we wish to follow your progress."

Vlad smiled to himself as he opened a drawer. "Oh, yes —it is necessary that you leave behind a . . . segment of yourself." The vampire selected a long scalpel from the drawer and tested its blade gently with a thumb. "But we'll replace it with something very special—to keep you on your toes, eh? If you muff your lines in a production I mount, you will, indeed, bomb." Paler grinned.

I: 3

THE SMELL of charred flesh hung heavy over the ruined nave while the villagers went about the grim work of hauling up corpses for the fire. Roald MacPherson stood nearby, occasionally ordering more wood tossed into the flames. His sword pulsed in his hand, ready to thrust at the least sign of enemy life.

Oliver Dolan sat upon a rotting log, his hands to his face. Penton hovered nearby, urging brandy upon the young man. Finally Oliver took a swallow, but he derived no warmth from the liquor. His bandaged hand was swollen and ached terribly. Snow still fell and the world was black and white save where daubs of blood had splashed the snow. Desolation had overcome Oliver Dolan—did death *have* to permeate his life so?

"After this, we should take a bit of a holiday," Caspar Penton murmured. He looked long at the sky. "Night's come awfully early."

"We started *much* too late." Oliver sighed. "No matter. The job is done. I just want to return to the village, have a hot bath, and go to bed."

"And we must see to that hand," Penton added.

"Yes."

"What do you make of it all, sir? Not a bit of wiring in the bloodsuckers. They're the real thing. And that MacPherson—how did he find us so fortuitously? We were goners, I tell you. Who is the chap?"

"Says he's the Angel of the Lord. But that sword of his is some kind of—what did Turner call it? Yes. A laser. I used one. Should have kept it, actually. I tossed it off in an emotional moment."

"Are you saying he's from some other world, like that lass Dubrelizy?"

"Like Anziel?" A small laugh escaped Oliver, but he felt a shred of wistfulness invade. "Not likely. No, Styx produced the fellow. God knows, it's got plenty of stuff in its grab bag." Exhaling a plume of white mist, Oliver stood, and called out: "That just about it, gentlemen? I'd like to finish this up."

31

One of the men by the trapdoor turned. "Just about. How're poor Renbard and Blake?"

"They'll be all right, I believe," Penton answered. "We've got them in the van."

"And the two dead?"

MacPherson turned and pointed toward the bonfire. "They must be burned."

There was a pause. "But what about their families? They deserve decent Christian burials, don't they?" The squat, beefy man stepped forward, blustering with indignation.

"They must be burned," MacPherson said firmly. "For their families' sakes. For all your sakes. The Lord will understand, and their souls will be as happy to have been released from ashes as from corpses."

The men muttered, but the response seemed mostly to be agreement. What they had seen that afternoon had given them much to ponder.

A muffled yell rose from the vault. With a flurry, the nearest to the trapdoor leaned down to listen, then straightened. "We've found another coffin! It's been locked fast."

"Bring it up," MacPherson directed gruffly. "I will deal with the inhabitant immediately."

Penton stiffened. "What ho! Perhaps we might squeeze some words from it before the sword descends. Give us an idea about what the devil's happening hereabouts."

"There's a thought," Oliver said, stalking forward immediately. "If we had an idea about who that statue yonder represents, we might have a clue that would give us a jump on these new creatures."

The townsmen grunted as they tugged at their load. Gradually, the end of a coffin rose into fitful firelight, then dropped heavily into the snow. A subtle cedar scent accompanied the gleaming box. A special coffin, then. Oliver touched the top with his good hand, and for a moment thought he detected a gentle surge of tickling *otherness* just on the verge of image, just on the edge of communication.

One of the men emerged from the vault and dusted the snow from his trousers. " 'Tis locked, as I said. Need a crowbar'n axe maybe. All the time we was sliding it toward the rope, there was this kind of whimper comin' out. Spooked me, I tell you."

Oliver nodded to Penton, who ran to their van.

A resonant voice sounded from behind Oliver. "It senses

its end. We must finish it, for while the blood is alive, it spreads."

The others were cowed, but Oliver spoke up. "Right, MacPherson. Now, you just tell us what you're about, fellow. We thank you for our lives, but admit to some curiosity about your costume and that fiery sword of yours. Where do you come from?"

MacPherson turned to the young man. "I do not know. I am Angel made flesh, that much I have within me. But God in his wisdom has cut from me my memory of Heaven or the wherewithal of my arrival here, perhaps so that during my mission I should not pine for my Heavenly home. Merciful is the Lord, may His name echo in the Heavens with praise. We should pray."

Oliver eyed the fellow suspiciously. "You're telling us that you've amnesia. You awoke someplace with this sword and a divine mission to destroy nightcreatures?"

"Vampires. Infected humans, not Satan's mandroids, who, though wretched in God's sight, do not carry this plague."

"When was all this?"

"Time is nothing to the Lord or His servants."

"Very well. If you don't remember *when*, surely you remember *where*."

"I do not, nor does it matter." The man glowered at Oliver and chided: "Where is your faith, lad? Why do you question the workings of the God you serve?"

"With all respect, sir, so many questions are floating about, I don't think God minds men asking a few now and then."

MacPherson shook his head gloomily. His hair was long and curled at the ends. He seemed all sticks and boards, angles and lines. His cheekbones were sharp, his cheeks sunken. He did not seem ever to blink. "Ours is not to question in this world where Evil reigns supreme. We can but follow the straight and narrow path over the chasm."

"How did you know we needed help?" a brave lad ventured from the ground surrounding the coffin.

"The path of infection had led me here. Your brothers of the town indicated where you had gone. The Lord bid me hasten."

The boy, younger than Oliver, shivered and said, "Well, praise the Lord for that."

Amens were muttered.

"Will you accompany us to the village?" Oliver said to the stranger.

"Those are my instructions. Ah—the instruments."

Huffing with exertion, Penton rejoined them with a crowbar and a hatchet. "Best I could do."

MacPherson nodded somberly. "Gentlemen. Do your duty"—he brandished the sword high—"and I shall do mine."

"I'm in charge here," Oliver stated brusquely. "Unless it proves necessary, you will *not* harm the inhabitant of this box until I give the command! We should at least interrogate the vampire before killing it." Glare met stare, and MacPherson muttered reluctant assent.

Penton handed the tools to the strongest and least weary of the bunch.

"Crowbar to the hinges, I should think," Penton said. It was quickly done. "Now," Penton ordered, "as one, dump it!"

The men obliged immediately, lifting the lid and turning the coffin over.

A female figure in flowing blue rolled into the snowbank and lay still, damp hair pasted against her face. Two red wounds marred an otherwise lovely throat. She moaned and shuddered like a child helpless in the cold.

Warmth stirred Oliver, and he sensed something vulnerable in his being. Such beauty in a world of black and white . . .

Oliver knelt beside the girl, felt her forehead. She was warm, temperature seemingly normal. His fingers found her lips and pried them gently apart. Her teeth were straight and white, not a fang among them. Oliver shrugged off his greatcoat and wrapped the limp form gently. "Penton, we must get her to the van! Well, don't just stand there! Do it, blast you."

"She is infected," MacPherson snarled, his Scots burr deeper with his anger. The townsmen stood fast. "We cannot take the—"

Oliver turned upon him. "You bloody ass! She's still human! The vampires hadn't killed her yet." He held up his bandaged hand. "If she's beyond hope, then so am I."

"Very well," MacPherson said, "but, look to your soul, man. That's what they want." He scowled at the girl. "Your soul." Coat and scarf swirling fluidly, he turned and walked to the fire and watched the bodies burn, arms on his chest, in a stance of righteous indignation.

Unaided, Oliver carried the unprotesting bundle to the van, then with Penton's assistance set her upon a cot. Bathed by light electric rather than fire, she looked even weaker and more helpless than before. Oliver slipped Penton's flask between her lips. She coughed, and Oliver suddenly found himself staring into depthless blue eyes.

"Pretty thing," Penton commented as he searched for something more appropriate in the cluttered medicine cabinet. "If you'd like me to have a look at her, sir . . . I've some experience with medicine."

"You think she'll come through, Penton?" Oliver could not contain the anxiety in his voice.

The older man doffed his coat and knelt by the girl. He took her pulse; opened an eyelid; examined the marks on her neck; listened to her breathe. Looking up at Oliver, he said, "Normally, my guess would be yes, she'd be fine. But this is no common malaise—infection, that MacPherson character said. Some sort of virus spread by vampires, that changes the dead into vampires."

"Yes. But only if you die. That must be it."

"We'll certainly have to query our attendant Angel further on the subject. For now, I suggest we wrap up our duties here and get this young lady to a warm house. There's nothing like the comforts of home—particularly a feather bed—to nurse a person back to health."

"I could use one of those as well." Oliver slumped into a chair, and thumbed idly at a control. The lighting muted a bit, softening the straight lines and angles of the van's interior. He tried to focus his thoughts upon the furnishings, and pretend he was in a comfortable, if tiny, Victorian parlor, but his attention strayed to the steering wheel, the controls, the electric motor, and the weapons in the teak cabinets.

Oliver had made some interesting discoveries in the van he'd inherited from Turner. They'd had such a short time together, he and Turner, yet the mandroid had five hundred years and more of experience that might have been passed down to Oliver, had the fellow survived. Soon, Oliver knew, he would have to find the headquarters of Turner's organization, the Holy Order to Preserve the Empire—HOPE.

Oliver selected a crystal and fitted it into a slot. Something fairly soft, and soothing. A Brandenburg concerto sweetened the air.

Penton slipped some medicine into the girl's mouth. "A

tonic for the blood," he explained as he dabbed with a silk handkerchief at the green rivulet on her chin. "There," he said, drawing the covers around the girl's neck. "That should do." But the image that superimposed itself over the girl in Oliver's mind was of Anziel, disheveled and disoriented. A rabbit hole opened in his thoughts, and he found himself musing about the Wonderland of feminine mystery. So soft and warm and promising . . .

A knock on the door roused Oliver. "I'll get it," Penton said. He crossed to the rear doors, peered through the peephole, then opened them to the squat man whose strength had proved so useful.

The man held his hat and worked it nervously between his hands. "Mr. Dolan, sir? About the girl—her name is Jennifer Eden."

"Indeed," Oliver said, rising. "She must have relatives. We must notify them immediately."

The man gestured to the roaring blaze. "Mother and father roast yonder. She's got no other kin. I knew her da, I did, and—" A kind of pathetic eagerness entered his eyes. "And I'd be glad to care for the poor thing."

"Your offer is appreciated," Oliver returned graciously. "For now, though, the inn will do. When she regains her faculties, she can decide what should be done." He stepped closer to the man, and his voice lowered. "I take it the entire family was kidnapped."

"Aye. They left for market one morning last week and never returned. A body can't trust the day no more." The man shook his head mournfully, as he turned away into the snowfall. "Truth to tell, young sir, if you tell the truth —that you killed Satan 'imself—then I wish you never had." His diminished form was outlined briefly by the orange of the fire. "You bloody opened all of Hell on us, 'aven't you?" The muttering voice waned into the night, and Oliver stood frozen in the doorway.

Finally a firm grasp on his shoulder pulled him in. "Come, sir," Penton said. "Let's have a closer look at that hand. Some astringent might be in order. Perhaps even stitches." Oliver allowed himself to be led back inside. Penton closed and bolted the doors and immediately began to fuss over his master.

"Penton, I think perhaps I should stop all this."

"All what, sir?" The last bit of bandage peeled off, and Oliver gave a start.

"This foolishness. I should just let Turner's ghost rest,

and give Styx over to whatever comes." His voice was a hollow monotone, echo of his doubt. "God knows, maybe I should just pray that Anziel brings her civilization here to gawk. Perhaps *they'd* do something about this mess." He shook his head sorrowfully. "Before, at least, Styx had some sort of order to its madness. Boundaries were observed, and if one was prudent in the night, life could be pleasant. Today it's province against province, freebooting day- and nightcreatures, and now this—this disease. It must have something to do with that vampire idol. But what can we do? I haven't five hundred years to work with as Turner had, nor Anziel's weapons. The people won't listen to me at all, and they believe only what they care to. To them it's still a world of magic, of good and evil."

"From what you've said about Anziel and galactic civilization, it doesn't sound as if mankind has made much progress in the mainstream, either. I think it unlikely she will return at all."

"I thought I could prepare Styx for that possibility," Oliver murmured. "But it's hopeless."

"One shouldn't make decisions in times of stress and fatigue, sir," Penton said, clucking over the bite marks. The bleeding had stopped.

"Awfully sorry, sir. And this iodine is going to hurt even more, I'm afraid."

"Is it absolutely necessary?"

"Better than MacPherson's sword."

"What?"

"Yes. He wanted to cauterize the wounds. Drive out the vampire venom, don't you know. I was supposed to hold you down while he did it."

"He had an inkling I wouldn't like that much, I take it."

"Fellow's a bit of a Calvinist. Mark my words, he'll be around for a while. I saw him staring at you quite strangely."

"Good Lord."

"Yes." Penton daubed the wounds with medicine. Oliver winced, but kept silent. "Rather like a proud father. Proud but disturbed."

"Father? No thanks!"

"Glum as a nun about not killing the girl, he is. He'll probably go off and flagellate himself in penitence. He's the type."

"If he's human."

Penton raised his eyebrows. "Ah, now. There's a thought.

You think he could be another stranded Victorian mandroid like Mr. Turner—or should I say, Mr. Wells."

"Geoffrey made no mention of him, and I think he'd have known of someone like Mr. MacPherson bouncing about."

"Could it be one of Satan's folk, confused?"

"Reversed polarity, you think?"

"Yes. Something like that. There's *evil* about that type— you know, the sort who'd burn a witch at the drop of a broomstick." Penton paused. "Sir, you once mentioned that Anziel lost her weapons when her horse threw her."

Oliver snapped his head back. "That's right! Perhaps he thought he'd found a Sword of Fire, like the angel guarding the Garden of Eden—demented, MacPherson thought it was sent by God. So there's the possibility even that he *is* human."

"Albeit deranged."

"Isn't that part of the definition? I'd not be surprised at any aberration in this absurd world."

"Have we descended even to *existentialism,* sir?"

Oliver shook his head as Penton began to rewrap the wound with fresh bandages. "You should be the master and I the manservant, Penton. I stand in awe."

"Ah, sir," Penton said. "But you have the money. And the mission. You don't know how much easier it is for us followers when we have noble leaders about."

Oliver snorted.

"Sir, self-deprecation serves a purpose only to a point."

"Wisdom from the fount?"

"Nothing less. For a price."

"I shall petition my father to give you a raise."

"I cannot pretend that would not be welcome," Penton said as he tied the final knot. "That should do. You'll have scars, but stitches won't be needed." He stood from his kneeling position. "Now I'll see to the horses."

"I'll go with you. You shouldn't be alone up there when you drive."

"Please. I'll be all right. We're part of a large group. I'd duck in here in a flash at first sight of trouble. Besides, with that hand what good would you be? Only hurt yourself more, sir." He looked over at the sleeping girl. "You look after the young lady. And you rest."

After Penton's departure, Oliver quickly convinced himself that the girl was well. She breathed evenly and fully, the swell of her breast was regular. Oliver touched the gold of her hair, once, softly.

He stared down at her for a long time.

The front hatch opened. "We're off, sir!"

"Right!" Oliver called back.

The hatch closed. The van jerked into motion. Oliver slouched down on the cushioned seat, thinking to doze off to the gentle lull of a Handel cassette.

But demon eyes stared at him from the night outside and the doubts swarmed in his soul; no sleep would come.

He retrieved headphones from the cabinet, popped the Bach tape and slid in some Handel.

"EVERY SCENE of every play must have a climax, Darkwing." Paler held a large hypodermic needle with both handles. He squeezed it slightly and fluid spurted. "In this scene, yours will be painless."

The jabberwock was already so full of drugs he was limp. Darkwing could barely discern the vampire before him. The aching drone remained, though. A liturgy, a dirge . . .

About him lay a vast chamber where bunsen burners flamed like votive candles at some black mass. It was Dr. Frankenstein's lab grafted to Dr. Jekyll's, furnished with random lots of supplies drawn from four centuries of scientific practice.

Vlad jammed the hypodermic needle into the jabberwock's soft underbelly and injected slowly. "You'll feel absolutely no pain, but you will retain consciousness. I appreciate appreciation."

The jabberwock could only voice monosyllabic protest: "What . . . 'ave . . . I . . . done . . . to . . . de . . ."

Extracting the needle, the doctor swabbed on alcohol. "Nothing. You just happened to be the nearest jabberwock. However, I am not without compassion." He puttered about a tray of surgical instruments. "You will do nothing you've never—you *have* killed humans before, have you not?"

"Only . . . when . . . necessary."

"A technicality. I know your nature, jabberwock, for I am its architect. But, *I* have need of your considerable talents and strengths; you realize I cannot take any chance."

"What . . . what . . . ?" A weary breath.

"Yes, that is a shame, Darkwing." For a moment, the vampire seemed genuinely sad. "A brilliant piece of bioengineering, that. And such a comfort. Hampton, you call yours? How clever. Actually, if I'd a choice I'd let you keep him. Alas, I have greater need for him than you. But you will not be without company." He indicated a round device upon the table beside him. "An explosive charge, Darkwing, with which you will be implanted—along with other items of interest. You, however, need only worry about going against my wishes, in which case . . ." Paler pushed an imaginary button in front of him: "I'll just have to find another jabberwock!"

He advanced with his scalpel.

Great teardrops welled from the jabberwock's limpid eyes.

"You'll not find surer hands to deal with electronics or flesh." He made a deep incision. "I say, your liver is rather off. When you return, I'll give you a new one. Remind me. And please lay off the alcohol. I want a healthy beast at my beck and call. Yes. Right." He wiped some sweat from his forehead.

He jerked out his hand, shook it. "Bastard bit me! Do tell him to cooperate, Darkwing."

"I . . . can't . . ." the jabberwock said. "Mind of . . . his own."

"Yes, that was my idea. But doesn't he do his job? Maintaining all that. Can't you tell him what to do?"

"I'll . . . try. . . ." The jabberwock closed his eyes, the hatred churning, and through the haze of drugs he thought, *Mate and pal, cooperate. I swear to you, you will be all right.*

Very well, but I shall miss you terribly, Darkwing.

And I you. Darkwing opened his eyes. "Just hold out your . . . hand . . . paler . . . bit . . . cold. Hampton . . . not . . . used . . . needs clothing."

The vampire thrust his arm once more into the belly. When the hand once more emerged, something stood on its palm. "Enchanting," Vlad said. "You know, it wouldn't have been possible without microminiaturization, Darkwing."

Standing upon his hand was a homunculus. But for its size—perhaps eight or nine inches tall—it would have been a perfect human male. It wore only shorts and a shirt, and a wealth of long black hair. Its voice was ready, piping: "Did I hear you mention clothing? I could do with some." His expression burned with sarcasm. "Oh, and I didn't bite you." He nodded back toward the cavity. "You stuck yourself—um, accidentally on one of my tools."

The vampire deposited the little man upon the table. Hampton slipped on trousers that proved baggy, and shirt and coat that he claimed were too tight. Then he gazed up at his nodding jabberwock, and pointed a tiny index finger at him. "What have you been pumping into Darkwing

41

here? I maintain him, and I don't like to see him screwed over."

"Drugs, harmless drugs. You both are too important to me to risk harming, I assure you of that. Now, as we'll have a great deal of time for discussion, I'll take you to your quarters and sew your host back up."

"Just tell me you're not going to hurt Darkwing. We've been together for a while."

"I assure you, Darkwing will not be harmed, and if all goes well you will be reunited quite soon. Come, now."

The homunculus stepped onto Vlad's waiting palm and was transported to a large black box. As he was lowered into the container, Hampton turned and for a moment the gazes of symbiont and host locked in open and mournful farewell. Darkwing could sense the nothingness within him. Only twice had they parted, but on both occasions for significant periods, when Hampton and some other homunculus-symbiont were paired in the production of a new jabberwock. However, those separations had merely been physical, for the two jabberwocks who contributed the material and the symbionts to construct another of their kind lingered in the place of "birth" to protect the newborn. But now the threat of permanent separation hovered.

The doctor closed the lid and saw that it was properly secured. He then turned swiftly to Darkwing.

"My friend, who knows better than I what pain you must be suffering now. Please believe me, the use to which I will put your companion is the very noblest, the most exciting experience Hampton will ever have." He shrugged. "Besides, you'll have *me* to keep you company now."

"What . . . do . . . you . . ."

"Mean?" The doctor strolled to a table. In its center stood a device that resembled a television surmounted by a periscope. He tapped the screen. "We shall see, Master Darkwing. We shall see."

OLIVER DOLAN opened his eyes. Shreds of dreams still clung. He recalled a river of blood flowing to some Final Sea.

But now it was light. Sunlight made the room bright. Oliver grew aware of the throbbing in his hand, and he recalled the bite of the vampire. But he lay comfortably swathed in sheets on one side of a huge, soft bed piled high with down blankets. Above him stretched oaken rafters. Sagging plaster walls were spiderwebbed with cracks. Recently whitewashed and clean, the room was, nonetheless, old.

The inn, thought Oliver. He did not remember arriving, but he was at the Courtyard Inn of Perth.

Oliver turned over, hugging the feather pillow under his head. Unworried now by doubts philosophical or ethical, inner conflict, or any earthly concern, he drifted between sleep and waking, eyes half open.

Beside him he noted another pillow. Peeking above the top of the pillow was a lock of long hair. A woman's hair . . .

A woman?

Oliver blinked. He pushed himself up. Yes. There, snuggled to his left, form unmistakable beneath the covers, face flushed a delicate pink, mouth in a baby's moue, was a woman, asleep. Red welts upon her neck now seemed less wounds than the result of a lover's ardor.

"Good God!" Oliver exclaimed. What was he doing here? What had happened. Several intriguing possibilities came to him almost immediately, bringing a blush to his face. Oliver swept off the covers to flee the embarrassing situation. However, he quickly drew the covers back. He was baby-bare.

The young woman stirred then and groaned, turning over and instinctively reaching for the warmth she sensed beside her. Her left arm clung about Oliver's neck and her soft face buried itself in his chest. She wore a long robe that felt warm and soft against Oliver's skin.

"Uh . . . I say—hullo?" Oliver gently, almost reluctantly,

attempted to pry the girl away. "I'm sorry, miss, but something is terribly wrong here. Please wake up."

Gummy eyelashes fluttered briefly, parted. Oliver found himself staring into blue irises. The pretty mouth worked, and the young woman said: "What? Don't wake me. I'm tired."

Eyes closed. Embrace re-emphasized itself; her left leg moved over Oliver's left. His mouth grew dry. He was quite awake.

"No, really. You must wake up. This just isn't—proper." He gently shook his companion by the shoulder.

Her eyes opened again, and she noted Oliver with open wonder but without shyness. "Oh. Who are you?" she asked sleepily. Then suddenly she realized their situation. "Oh my." She slipped to her side of the bed, holding the covers close.

"My name is Oliver Dolan, and I must apologize!" Realizing that most of his chest was exposed, he slunk neck-deep under the sheets.

"Whatever for?"

Oliver paused. "I—don't know."

"Where are we? I remember . . . I remember a sleigh ride on a cold, bright morning, and mittens, and hot tea in a thermos. Mother and Father were laughing as we slipped along . . . and then"—her expression grew solemn—"I don't remember." Her hand reached out and touched Oliver on the shoulder. "Was there some kind of . . . accident?"

"Not precisely."

"Oh, dear, my neck," a slim hand touched the wounds. "It hurts dreadfully!"

"An accident. Yes," Oliver said. "Something like that!"

Her eyes brightened. "And you saved me!"

"Well, perhaps, but it's not what you—"

"And I was dying of frostbite. And the only warmth at hand was that of your own body!" Her delivery was that of a romantic enthusiast. It seemed she could hardly contain herself from consuming him with kisses, but a lifetime's Victorian inhibition bound Oliver, tripping up his words and his emotions.

"Not quite," he finally managed to return.

"Whatever happened, I'm most grateful."

"I—uh—I find it quite awkward here. I don't even know you and somehow we're sharing a bed. I confess, I'm a little at a loss."

"You mean, I didn't have frostbite?"

Oliver was able only to shake his head.

"Oh, dear. Is it possible we were gripped by passion so consuming it burned our memories away? I rather hoped I'd remember the first time I slept with a man."

"Of course not! Why, that's ridiculous!" Oliver sputtered.

"You don't like being here with me?"

"I love being—no. No, dammit, that's not what I mean. I mean, this is just not the thing. There's been a ghastly misallocation of sleeping space. I would *never* enter a young lady's"—he coughed—"bed."

"This *is* a very nice bed. Is there something wrong with *me?*"

"I don't even *know* you!" Oliver raised his arms in exasperation. "There is something called morality. Decorum —the system by which we order our lives."

"My name is Jennifer Eden. Now, we must be practical about this, Oliver. What we did last night has little bearing on our lives, or on this *morning,* as a matter of fact. We must be adult about this. We can't just sweep this under the cover—" She smiled, faintly embarrassed. "I mean rug."

"Look, Jennifer, we have much to talk about, and this is not the place."

"So leave. Go. Depart. Get thee hence, Oliver Dolan. Boys have been trying for my bed since I budded breasts, and the first to make it can't wait to get out! Men!"

"You don't understand."

"I understand that you're acting very strangely."

His face quite red, he leaned over and whispered, "I haven't anything on."

She raised her eyebrows. "My goodness. Yes, perhaps you should go. I'll turn my head."

"Thank you."

Oliver glanced around the room. Hanging over a wooden chair in the far corner were his clothes, still soiled. "I *do* appreciate your cooperation," he said.

"My eyes are shut very tight," she said. "I can't see a thing."

Exasperated, he peeled back the covers. But, as Oliver's feet touched the cold floor, the chamber door swung slowly open.

He jumped back into bed.

"That was quick," Jennifer said.

"Someone's coming in."

"And we're compromised! Well, Oliver, there's nothing for it. We'll just have to get married."

"What?"

As the door came to rest against its stop, a large figure entered carrying a great wooden tray topped with all manner of covered dishes. "Good morning," the man said. "I hope you both slept well."

"I demand to know what is going on here! Why weren't we given separate chambers?" Oliver was quite beside himself. *Compromised!*

The man, tall and horribly scarred, walked forward unsteadily and his uneven gait threatened the precarious balance of the items upon the tray. The room suddenly smelled of breakfast, and despite himself, Oliver realized he was ravenous. He was a bit cowed by the size of the visitor, who must have measured close to seven feet. The scars were peculiarly placed, as if the result of surgery. The nose was broken, the skull misshapen, the teeth jagged—but friendly eyes and a smile softened these horrific aspects.

But at Oliver's continued remonstrations, the expression became troubled.

"Ah. Your manservant explicitly stated that you were to be placed in feather beds. As we have but one feather bed, and as Mr. Penton had already retired to his basement room, I thought it expedient to place you both in the same bed. You made no objection, sir."

"I was bloody well konked out! I hope you realize what a situation you have placed us in, sir! And why did you remove my clothing?"

"Soaked through and through, sir."

"It would appear that the only person whom this has troubled is yourself, Oliver," Jennifer said, cocking her head inquisitively. "Why is that?"

Oliver opened his mouth to explain, but could not. He'd lived all his life armored by conventional behavior. One had to have codes, proper structure.

Jennifer turned to the scarred man. "You did well, Mr. Creech. A warm presence beside me did me no end of good. Practicality first, I've always said. Now, I see you've brought breakfast. I confess I'm famished."

" 'Tis a welcome thing to have you so, Miss Eden. You were a sore fright last night, you were indeed. So very pale and shuddery." Clucking, he maneuvered to a side table and set down the tray. "How do you feel now?"

"Quite well, thank you, Mr. Creech. I have a number of things to speak to you two gentlemen about, but nothing that cannot wait until I've had a cup of tea."

"You two know each other?"

"Oh, yes. Most everyone hereabouts knows Mr. Creech."

"Everyone has been most kind to poor Creech," the man said, adding milk and sugar. "Do pass this to the lady, Mr. Dolan. Yes, when I showed up they took me in and treated me quite proper, despite my background."

"Background?"

"Aye. Used to be what they call a nightcreature, I did."

"*Do* be careful, Oliver. You've almost dumped it in my lap!"

"Nightcreature?" Oliver eyed the fellow warily.

"Yes. Modeled, I believe, upon Mary Shelley's Franken-stein monster. Rather badly, I fear. More monster than the Prometheus fashioned after Percy Bysshe Shelley in the book. But man enough to need the company of other humans."

"Which explains your actions last night. No normal Victorian would shove a naked man in bed with a lady not his wife!"

Jennifer sipped daintily at her tea. "Victorian? What is a Victorian?"

"You've heard of the Great Queen of Legend?"

"Yes, of course, but only in tales told to children. Surely she wasn't real?"

"Her name was Victoria and she was a computer simulacrum who modeled herself on the original Queen Victoria of England. She created the Second Victorian Empire throughout space, much as the first Victoria presided over the seas. She codified our laws and morals and reinstituted Christianity. She formed Styx, modeling it after an ideal-ized earlier England unblemished by industry, managed from an underground computer control center. But the man in charge of the system became deranged and took control of it, meshing himself with the computer. Believing himself to be Satan incarnate, he transformed Styx into Nightworld and created the nightcreatures. The cyborg reigned five hundred years before Geoffrey Turner and I destroyed him. All we are now stems from Victorian civili-zation, and thus I call us Victorians."

47

Jennifer looked imploringly to Mr. Creech. "What manner of madman have you put in my bed, Mr. Creech?"

"No, honestly, I can prove everything. Turner was a remnant of the Victorian Space Empire. A mandroid, modeled after the Victorian H. G. Wells. I can show you his transportation—it's how we reached here from the vampire vaults—"

"Vampires?" The humor in her eyes vanished, to be replaced by fear. "My parents?" She felt her neck, and the cup began to shake. "The accident!"

Mr. Creech bowed his head sorrowfully. "I'm afraid they're gone, Miss Eden. Just as you'd be if it weren't for Mr. Dolan here, and Mr. Penton."

"Dead?" Oliver could only look away, confused by a blend of embarrassment and sympathy.

"Yes," Mr. Creech said. His eyes were moist. "That is what Mr. Penton says."

"I remember some of it now. I remember teeth, and I remember cold. I remember . . . I remember the blood bond."

"What?"

She shook her head. "Just images. Impressions. No more. That's all . . . Oh. Oh, dear. Father. Mother."

"The creatures that did this have been destroyed," Oliver said, deeply troubled and not entirely certain why. "We will see that you recover from your wounds. I myself was attacked."

He held out his hand as if to show her the bandage, but somehow the gesture was deeper than that. He wanted to comfort her somehow, and yet he could not.

Drawing up her knees, she said, "Gentlemen, would you please leave now? I will take breakfast later." Mr. Creech seemed almost to writhe with sorrow.

"You're young, sir. Can you comfort her. Poor Creech is all thumbs with women."

"No. She needs to be alone for a time. Just fetch my clothes. We'll check on her later. I need to see to the van and my manservant." Oliver grabbed the proffered clothing from Creech, slipping on only his trousers and shirt.

He paused before leaving and glanced at Jennifer Eden. She was curled into a ball beneath the covers and her eyes, those pure blue eyes, stared sightlessly into the distance. *All curls and curves,* he thought, *all softness and warmth, all alone.* "Beautiful," he murmured.

He pulled at Mr. Creech's sleeve. "Leave the tray. Jennifer might want something after she's had opportunity to compose herself."

Mr. Creech nodded and they quietly departed.

They had kippers for breakfast. And fried eggs and thick slabs of bacon and hefty hunks of bread. At intervals along the table were pots with fresh golden butter, and all manner of pastries abounded, steamy hot. They ate within the private dining room of the rambling inn, a comfortable chamber stocked with all manner of Victorian odds and ends. Stuffed animal heads hung from the walls, alongside portraits, candlesticks, and archaic electric light fixtures.

Mr. Creech labored over a slab of ham with knife and fork. He had all the dexterity of a bear wearing mittens. Eventually he peered hopefully at the matronly woman across the table and was rewarded with a scolding.

Mrs. Creech then turned to Oliver and Caspar Penton. "You must excuse my husband. His mind has marvelous possibilities, and his strength is unmatched in the entire countryside, but his former . . . ah, employment quite deprived him of facility at detail work. More scones, Mr. Penton?"

Eyes bright and innocent, Mr. Creech said, "I was very good at throwing little girls in lakes and strangling women!"

"Yes, and we've no more of that since we've reformed—true, Mr. Creech?" She was a tiny woman, rounded all about with too much sampling of her own cooking, but she radiated authority.

Penton politely accepted another scone. "I would imagine that Mr. Creech's behavior had nothing to do with his own will, and as soon as Satan's death loosed Hell's control, Mr. Creech's own natural good nature flowed freely."

The middle-aged woman stiffened. "Not bloody likely. 'Twas the fear of God I put in that reformed his ways! Mr. Creech still twitches with Lucifer's evil from time to time, but His will has been done and Mr. Creech has joined the Blessed Flock of the Repentant." She softened as she looked at her husband, leaning over and patting him on his scarred hand. "But he does have much love in him, the big fellow."

"When she speaks of evil, she speaks of my unnatural affection for Shelley and the Romantic poets. I leave the little girls and women alone, nor have I a single thought to

49

return to my wretched ways!" The reformed monster grinned.

"It is not the poetry of God, Mr. Creech. But the Truth will someday convince you."

"I sang of the dancing stars,/I sang of the daedal Earth," quoted Penton. "And of Heaven—and the giant wars,/And Love and Death, and Birth—"

"Yes, yes," said Mr. Creech, quite excited. "'Hymn of Pan'!" He rolled his great eyes with great joy. "Lovely, lovely."

The assembled company gradually sank into joyous though unruly repast, and Oliver's mind ranged back upon family breakfasts in great drafty chambers, his father, Viscount Dolan, dour, mother glacial. Thought of his dead mother brought a pang. And his father might as well have been dead—though the man still ruled, he could not accept what had happened to his world, nor would he accept the mission of truth that his son had chosen. Already, no longer separated by the threat of Nightworld's creatures, the simple and independent provincial governments of Styx had begun to regroup into more powerful structures, combining armies and minds into would-be nations with conflicting interests. Wars were inevitable upon the continent. Who knew what was happening on the rest of the planet? Styx was a large enough world, and five hundred years of nightcreature depradations had fragmented a previously homogeneous culture. It was all too complicated to dwell upon. Of the myriad vagabond nightcreatures, some, like Mr. Creech, managed to find homes, others joined the armies or scavenged—or killed, as of old. Unfortunately, Satan's death allowed the last to apply cunning to what had been a mechanical process hampered by formal and inefficient restraints.

Oh, Anziel, Oliver thought ruefully. *Perhaps I should have left with you.*

Oliver's reverie was interrupted suddenly by the vigor of his companion's gaming.

"Lamia!" Mr. Creech cried, lurching back and forth with excitement. "John Keats! 'She was a cordian shape of dazzling hue/Vermilion spotted, golden green and blue.'"

Mrs. Creech leaned over and struck him gently upon the arm, staring at him insistently. "Mr. Creech! Eat your eggs before the yolks clot!"

Blowing on his tea, Penton leaned back in his chair. "Absolutely—Lamia." Oliver noted that his man's eyes were on the entrance to the kitchen. " 'She seemed, at once, some penanced lady elf,' " the manservant quoted. " 'Some demon's mistress, or the demon's self!' "

Oliver looked to where Penton's eyes had trained themselves. At the sagging doorway stood Jennifer Eden in clean woolens, her hair freshly washed.

"Good day!" she said. Her voice had a forced gaiety. "Might I take some breakfast with you? I'm quite famished."

Mrs. Creech rose quickly, matronly mountain of concern. "Dear girl! Of course." She bustled over and folded about Jennifer with a motherly kiss and hug. "What would you like? Something light?"

"Oh, whatever everyone else is having will do quite well."

"Now, if the kippers and the eggs are cold, I must make some more."

"Still warm, Mrs. Creech," Caspar Penton pronounced.

Jennifer accepted just a "little bit" of everything, except for muffins and jam. Of those she took two, explaining, "I have rather a sweet tooth."

"Sweetness in a woman. An admirable quality." Penton sat and addressed himself once more to his kipper. "An excellent meal, Mrs. Creech. How much more worthy is one who gives sustenance than we who merely take."

Mr. Creech produced another quote past a full mouth: " 'She found me roots of relish sweet/And honey wild and manna dew.' Keats. 'La Belle Dame Sans Merci.' "

Mrs. Creech proceeded to berate her husband.

Stifling a giggle, Jennifer whispered, "How comforting are life's inanities."

"How tragic its insanities," Oliver said.

She looked at him. "Keats. Shelley? Lord Bryon himself?" Her blue eyes held an exciting wordless challenge. "Or merely Oliver Dolan."

Oliver met the stare with affected effrontery. "Less the adverb, madam, you will find your answer."

She broke eye contact. "Sorry. Uncalled for."

"At times so is *all* conversation," Oliver said.

"But it comforts, doesn't it?"

"And occasionally hurts. We wield it so poorly," Penton said, interrupting. "The slings and arrows are often not of misfortune, but of language. How fascinating yet imperfect a tool of communication it is. It is armor and silk, sword and kiss."

"You have another suggestion?" Oliver said.

Penton drained his tea, then said, "We must live with what we have, no? Sometimes it is more than we think it is." He put down his cup. "Well. I must see to the van and some horses. Power's down a bit, and I imagine you would like to depart for home soon. We must see to your wound."

"I—I believe I need another day's rest, if that is all right with our hosts," Oliver said. He could not bear the idea of leaving Jennifer so soon.

Mrs. Creech was finishing painstakingly brushing off her skirt. "Stay as long as you like, gentlemen. Our debt is so great—"

"Besides, we *like* you very much!" Mr. Creech blurted.

"Very well, sir," Penton said, clearly disapproving.

"Excellent. We have much to discuss, anyway. This is as good a time as any to lay the seeds for a better relationship between our respective duchies. Perhaps the Duke of Perth will take kindly to certain subjects I wish to bring to his attention."

"Oh, I'm sure he'd very much like to speak with you, Oliver."

"Nonetheless, I shall see to the van," Penton said, and proceeded out the doorway. Unexpectedly, Penton's voice rang from the passage. "Good God, man! Have a care with that thing. You almost sliced my nose off! What have you got the bleeder *on* for?"

An unmistakable voice returned, "God's light must shine in the presence of evil."

"Well, turn it off before you hurt somebody."

MacPherson erupted into the kitchen, sword unrepentently ablaze. When he saw Jennifer at the table, he brandished his weapon before her.

"Who is that?" she asked, cringing against Oliver.

"Chap who saved our lives last night."

"Not very pleasant, is he?"

Mrs. Creech strode up to her newly arrived guest. "Mr. MacPherson, I do not think the sword is necessary."

"I'll hold her," Oliver volunteered. "Won't let her get you!"

MacPherson scowled, and reluctantly switched off his sword. He did not, however, sheath it.

"Mr. Dolan. I have been exploring the lair of the vampire folk."

"Well, have a seat and something to eat and tell us about it all!"

MacPherson nodded and sat stiffly in the wooden chair. He and Mrs. Creech eyed one another uneasily. "Do have some tea, Mr. MacPherson. Warm you up a bit."

MacPherson's mouth lost its rigidity. "This fleshly form *does* have a taste for earthly tea." His eyes sparkled a bit as he spied the tray of muffins, but he said nothing. Mrs. Creech perceived his interest and promptly insisted that he partake. MacPherson ate with relish and slurped tea with something like human enthusiasm. Between bites he spoke, careful not to look at Jennifer.

"Nigh dawn I rode back to be sure we had burned the lot. Could na' sleep." MacPherson loosened his scarf, then seemed to remember that his head was covered in the presence of women. He promptly removed the wide-brimmed black hat and placed it by his feet. "First, the chapel lair of the creatures. To be brief, I found another exit. Secret panel."

"To where?" Oliver asked.

"Oh, simply to a door farther on in the woods."

"And you followed it?"

"Of course."

"All by yourself?" Jennifer was sincerely impressed. "How brave of you, Mr. MacPherson."

The man smiled a bit, then recovered his poise. "At the end of the tunnel, the door was hidden by bushes. Beyond I found fresh footprints."

"But it snowed yesterday."

"Precisely, lad. The snow stopped late into the night. One of the creatures escaped! Evidently it concealed itself in the tunnel until we departed, and then fled. I suspect it is returning to its master—the subject of the idol—to report. As you know, the evil of vampirism spreads with the creature's bite. I have reason to suspect that the individual represented by the statue is the originator of the disease. Perhaps even Satan's present incarnation."

"But I *killed*—" Oliver caught himself, not wanting to argue. "Very well. Just who is this fellow? And what exactly are the conditions and qualities of vampirism. I admit, the young lady and I are most interested, since we ourselves have been infected."

"Ah, you hardly, Master Dolan. The young lady more so, I fear. I can see it in her eyes, though I do not believe she is in immediate danger. From my experience, however, it seems necessary that an individual expire before the full vampiric spirit takes hold. The infected are in a twilight territory. This vampire 'god,' whatever his name is, cannot control the infected. Only the dead. The *living* dead. Their wills are given over to him, and they are his servants. It is he that I seek. In the meantime I hack away branches in search of the trunk."

"What do you plan to do next?" Oliver asked.

"I confess, I do not know. I have not heard the will of God."

"God *talks* to you?"

"Of course."

"Can others hear?"

"No. It happens inside of me." Suddenly austere and forbidding once more, he pushed aside his half-eaten second muffin. "I must go."

He stood and started walking for the door. Oliver put a hand to his arm to detain him. "Hold a moment, man. I've a thousand questions to ask you."

Roald MacPherson turned and looked at Oliver, and there seemed an honestly troubled expression in the man's face. "I must go now and speak with my God." He pushed away Oliver's hand and stomped off.

The kitchen experienced a moment of silence.

"He's a mystery, no question. If only the mystery would talk more. I'm not sure if he's good for us or bad," Oliver mused.

"How can you say that, Oliver?" Jennifer said. "He saved your lives, didn't he?"

"Yes, and he bloody well wanted to hack off your head, woman." Oliver immediately regretted the anger.

Touching her throat, Jennifer said, "So that is how you saved my life."

"Don't think about it," said Oliver.

Mrs. Creech, however, was scandalized. "I can't believe a man of God, like Mr. MacPherson, would harm our Jenny!"

"Men of God have been known to do worse things," Oliver muttered. "But now, Jenny, I see you've finished your breakfast. Can we see about meeting the few important people you promised, hmm?"

"I think that can be arranged. But let me help Mrs. Creech clean up first. She was such a dear to—"

"Stuff and nonsense, girl! You'll do nothing of the sort. You're our guest, and besides, you're not strong enough for such work. And I have Mr. Creech to help me with such things—don't I, Mr. Creech?"

But Mr. Creech was unmoving, staring at the floor with the resignation of a prisoner with a life sentence.

"Mr. Creech! You know you must help with all the duties of this establishment."

"Yes, dear. I know. I know."

Mrs. Creech smiled victoriously up at Oliver and Jennifer. "Now you two be off and attend your business. Life must go on."

THE SKY WAS growing dark and a winter wind drove from the northeast, pushing swirls of biting snow before it.

A sled cut along the frozen roadway, and, from time to time, a whip would snap above the team that pulled it. Save for the wind whir, the merry tinkle of sleigh bells, and the hiss of metal on ice, all was silent. Suddenly the driver stood and cracked his whip twice. "You may halt!"

The pack trotted to a stop. The leader stood and unhitched his harness, cursing foully. "Daft trip. 'Bout froze me tail off!" His voice was more articulate growl than the Queen's English.

Vlad Paler removed his furs and called from the sled. "Big thermos of hot chocolate here for you chaps if you'd like some."

A particularly big nightcreature reared up on his hind legs and struck together the cleats upon his front limbs. In addition to its fur, each of the team wore coat and goggles. The big beast stamped his feet and shivered in canine fashion, spraying his neighbors with ice and snow clumps. "Didn't expect this sort of thing when I signed up. An' we got to go back i' the dead o' night! Need more than bloody lukewarm cocoa!"

The dark man flipped down his hood and nonchalantly picked about in the back of the sled. "Well, I did bring some sandwiches. That will have to do, I fear. Help yourselves while I'm gone. I shan't be long."

Muttering, Barktooth—the pack leader—turned around and headed for a nearby tree. The big werewolf, however, stood apart from the eight others. "What's to prevent us leaving your arse right 'ere? Headin' back ourselves."

Vlad Paler was retrieving a large cloth-covered box from the rear of the sled. "Ah, I've other servants who would retrieve me. And, Bloodbreath, who'll keep you for the winter? Can *you* afford the price of fresh red meat in these uncertain times? And what insurance do you have I'll not search you out and kill you after a round of exquisite torture?"

Bloodbreath snarled and licked his fangs. "I tell ye, I've half a mind to—"

"To *what,* cur?"

"Wouldn't rile 'im, guv'nor," one of the other werewolves whispered. "Nasty one, that."

Vlad Paler turned his head to the darkening sky and laughed.

With the pack leader's attention elsewhere, Bloodbreath concluded he might find support among the team. Rebellion was not apparent in their lupine aspects, but neither was loyalty.

He turned to Paler. "I'm going to eat your heart for supper!"

Perhaps five yards separated them. The spikes on the werewolf's hands shone dully as they flashed toward their victim.

Paler yanked up the left sleeve of his well-cut coat and his floppy French cuffs, to reveal a number of studded bands upon his wrist. He selected one and gingerly tapped it twice.

Bloodbreath seized his head; his eyes bulged most horribly; blood ran along a hairy chin. Gurgling, the werewolf fell to his knees. Paler ducked behind the sled, then called out, "Do stand back, chaps. I don't want to lose anyone else. There'll be—"

Bloodbreath's head exploded.

The carriage and the white of the snow were splattered. The body, hands missing as well as head, jerked and spasmed to a stand. Pieces of bone and metal in jagged disarray showed where the neck had been.

Paler peeked over the side of the carriage. "Shrapnel."

The decapitated body stepped forward once, then fell, smoking, into the snow.

Paler looked up brightly. "Well, then. There'll be more than sandwiches for you lads!"

The werewolves stood quite still while Barktooth walked slowly back from his tree.

Paler went about his business, stepping out of the carriage, hauling the box behind him. "Barktooth? Did you not inform Mr. Bloodbreath of the implant effected in employees below Grade Seven during their pre-employment physical examination?"

The werewolf stiffened. "I—I forgot, sir."

Reaching down, Paler selected a shotgun, electrostaff, and a pair of fist-sized spheres. He checked that there were shells in the breech, and put a handful in his side pocket along with the two spheres. "Just as well, Mr. Barktooth. He was more trouble than he was worth."

The werewolf relaxed noticeably.

Paler hefted the large box to his shoulder and began to ascend the incline into a copse of snow-laden trees.

"But sir!" Barktooth called. "Bloodbreath was our strongest. It will be hell on the return—"

"The load will be lighter." Paler inclined his head toward the box. "This will not be returning." Not waiting for a reply, he headed up the mountain.

The pack watched his departure for a minute, then trotted toward the sled for hot chocolate, and a bite of warm dinner.

The path had changed somewhat in the century and a half since Paler had last traveled it. Vines and brambles had overgrown much, and Paler was frequently forced to detour. Strengthened by his own internal machinery, he did not much mind the strenuous climb.

The sun finally set, and the stars faded in accompanied by Charon's sister, Athena, full in the sky. As he walked, Paler hummed to himself.

At a very steep section of his climb, up an icy cliff face, Paler stopped a moment to rest. Immediately, he heard the crunch of snow somewhere behind. He was being followed by something.

He lifted the black cloth covering and spoke into one of the tiny air holes. "What ho, captive Hampton. Sitting comfortably?"

"Hardly," returned a voice. "Cold. Damned cold."

"Not for much longer. Warmth awaits, I assure you." He rubbed some of the chill from his nose and patted his leather gloves together. "I say, have you any brandy left?"

"Drank it all."

"Ah."

"Drunker than a wine-vat worm."

"Would you like some more? We've a bit more snow to slosh through. Gets colder, the higher we go."

"You bet."

"Hold your cup beneath the center hole." Paler poured and dark gold brandy overflow dripped from the box. "A cupful should do it. Don't want you to pass out on me," the vampire murmured to himself. "Wouldn't do at all."

"Health and happiness, bloodsucker!"

"Absolutely." Paler returned the toast cheerfully, then

took a long pull at the flask. "You know, I'm not quite sure *which* I like better." He flicked his pink tongue at his canines appreciatively.

The snow glistened with moonglow. Stooped, warped trees with only snow for foliage clustered about some rocks only a few feet distant.

"Vare are vee going, Herr Paler."

"Shut up for a moment, will you."

"Can't I even talk?"

"I think I heard something before. I'd like to have a go at hearing again."

"Oh. Bloody marvelous!" However, Hampton did still his tongue.

Vlad Paler took off his top hat and cupped his ears to catch the faintest scrap of odd noise.

It came almost immediately: a scrape. Like claw against wood. And then a *shuffling*. A squeaky mutter. A whispered "Shussh!"

Paler flipped the safety off the shotgun. "Greetings, visitors. Imagine, a chance encounter like this on the slope of a forsaken mountain."

"Damn." A faint mutter, and then a muffled yelp as the mutterer was painfully silenced. At least two of them, then.

"You can speak then! What have you to say for yourselves."

His sharp eyes picked out a movement in the shadows below.

A voice emerged, all scraggly and swooping in pitch. "Hullo. We are weary travelers. Weary, *hungry* travelers."

"Ha ha! I thought as much. And you seek to dine on me!"

"Sir! You malign us! We but thought that the box you carry might contain a few crumbs for our empty stomachs!"

"Why, if *that* is all you want, join me for a rewarding repast."

"Paler? You're going to *feed* me to those things." Hampton was distraught.

"Would you keep still!" whispered Paler harshly.

Two voices buzzed below. The one which had spoken to Paler rose with anger and challenge. Paler heard the thuck of fist on flesh, then a figure loped into the moonlight, gangly arms dragging in the snow.

"My dear brother Stan will retrieve your kind offering."

Paler squinted down to make out the form better. Yes.

Horns atop a bizarre visage, sharp fangs. A barbed tail rode low between its legs. "Ah! Demons! What a pleasure. But you must both come, I do long for company."

The voice spoke out in anger. "Call us demons no longer. Satan's appellation is repellent to our sensibilities. We are known as the Brotherhood of Overmen. My name is Elmo." A shrill note of pride filled the creature's voice.

"Overmen, indeed. Well, all I can say is—oops." Paler squeezed the trigger of the shotgun. The blast knocked Stan the Overman off his hooves and pushed him a good five yards, trailing all manner of entrails, biological and mechanical. He rolled to a stop in the snow.

"Stan!" cried the shrill voice of Elmo.

"I do say! So sorry. My finger slipped."

"You piece of harpie dung!" cried the upset voice of Elmo the Overman. "You blew Stan away!"

"I *am* sorry. By the way, why have you started to circle above me? You were coming for your treat from a different direction?"

"I—er."

"Well, no matter. Actually, what I meant to tell you after you arrived here was that I haven't a thing in the box."

A relieved sigh sounded from within.

"Then you lied! You wanted to lure us out!"

"A man can't be too careful. I was about to say, friend Overman, that I came in a sled with a number of servants, who are presently dining. If you'd like, you may join them for a few scraps."

"Indeed! I *am* quite hungry!"

"Excellent. Perhaps we shall meet later."

The voice raised with curiosity. "Are you going to the Warm Springs Cavern up yonder, per chance?"

"Why, yes, I am. Why do you ask?"

The creature was hard pressed to contain a giggle. "Very well, friend stranger. But what is your name, that your companions will welcome me?"

"My name is Vlad Paler, friend Overman. Just tell them that Vlad Paler has sent you—"

A giggling form darted deeper into the shadows. Gradually the thrashings of its passage died away.

Paler grinned maliciously. "—for *dessert*. Your welcome will be warm, I'm sure."

"CAN I TEMPT you young people with some cherry pie?"

"Oh, dear, I don't believe I can force another thing down after that marvelous dinner," Jennifer protested.

"I fear I am all too open to temptation, Mrs. Creech." Oliver's stockinged feet were toasting pleasantly before the hearth. He was at ease after a productive day in the company of Jennifer and the town leaders. The evening meal, ham and trimmings, lay comfortably in his stomach, well mixed with strong ale. A full tankard sat by his elbow.

"Perhaps Jennifer can be persuaded by a dollop of fresh hot custard!" Mrs. Creech's eyes gleamed playfully.

Jennifer sat up, comforter slipping to her slim waist. "Custard!"

Mrs. Creech winked at Oliver as she began to slice the pie. "I know young Jenny's appetites, I do!"

"Custard!" Jennifer repeated.

"Yes, dear, warm and dripping and tasty. That is, if Mr. Creech ever arrives."

Jennifer bounced a bit on the cushion. "Father used to make custard on special occasions. I used to lick the bowl!" Her expression changed as her grief was recalled, and she leaned back, pulling the comforter to her chin.

Agitated, Mrs. Creech stalked away, rubbing her hands upon her white linen apron. "Mr. Creech! Mr. Creech! Where in creation are you!"

"I know how it is," Oliver whispered to Jennifer. "You'll feel better in a week or so."

"You lost your parents?"

"No. My mother. To a dragon."

"Here I am feeling sorry for myself, and you've had a wretched experience, too."

Oliver nodded.

Mr. Creech suddenly lumbered into the room, clumsily brandishing a mixing bowl and spoon. Mrs. Creech nipped at his heels. "—And the pie is supposed to be on the bottom." He carefully placed the bowl of custard upon the table.

"I'm sure everything will be quite fine," Oliver interjected, but Mrs. Creech would have none of it.

"He can't do anything right." She dabbed at the corner of an eye with the tip of her apron.

"The eggs, Mrs. Creech," Mr. Creech reminded forlornly. "There was a terrible problem with— But it tastes quite right! Worth the wait, I'll warrant, Mr. Dolan." He glanced toward Oliver for support.

"I really think that you're putting too much importance upon the whole thing," Jennifer stated emphatically. "You have been more than kind to both of us."

Mrs. Creech stamped her foot and pouted. "You just don't understand. I can't get an ounce of efficiency from him!"

"My dearest . . ." the giant said, gently moving to her. His hands slipped under her arms, and suddenly the small woman was hoisted to face Mr. Creech nose to nose. Thick tendons tensed. A stern smile betrayed crooked teeth. "My darling Mrs. Creech. Shut up!"

A pallor crept over Mrs. Creech's usually rosy cheeks. Her body went limp. "Yes, Mr. Creech," she murmured.

"There's a dear." He kissed her upon the nose and set her back down. "Now, I think the young folks would like to be alone in the parlor for a while. Why don't we go down to the inn and attend to the customers."

She nodded. They departed with murmured adieus.

"Well, then," Oliver said brightly, "I believe you mentioned custard!"

"I believe I did."

They fell to eating in silence as the fire spat and crackled before them, radiating light and heat in almost equal proportion.

Oliver felt an astonishing lack of tension in her presence. Their words and their silences seemed to mesh, their presences complementary to one another's.

It had been so throughout the day.

The town council, led by the local ruler, the Duke of Perth, had heard Oliver's report and thanked him for his efforts on Perth's behalf.

Oliver then took the opportunity to explain to the council the military situation upon Styx as he saw it.

For this he produced a map displaying all the information that he had been able to obtain about Styx's boundaries and states. Before the destruction of Satan, the land had been mock-feudal, governed—if at all—by city-states, none of which could be called a kingdom, because the governing units had to be small enough to be effectively walled against the nightcreatures that stalked the lands between sundown and dawn.

Such was no longer the case. All over Styx states were flexing their muscles, some augmenting their military manpower with rogue nightcreatures, who had little motive to avoid what to humans would be considered useless bloodshed.

Finally, Oliver mentioned the rise of the mysterious vampire lord and suggested that Perth ally itself with Fernwold, his father's Duchy, which would then send an ambassador to discuss a mutual defense agreement, trade pacts, and a congress to determine goals the provinces might have in common.

The Duke of Perth readily agreed to such a meeting, and questions had flown freely from the council. Oliver answered them as best he could, dispelling much doubt and supernatural misunderstanding concerning the nightcreatures and their origins.

"One last thing," he had concluded. "I assure you, just as everything I have said concerning the nightcreatures is true, so is this: we are but one planet of many populated by humankind. Previously, the humans of other worlds had no idea we existed. They do now. Vessels from these other worlds may land on Styx at any time. You must be prepared to change once more when this happens."

The council members huffed and puffed about how content they had been before, then the discussion moved on to less weighty topics. By early afternoon the session had been adjourned, so Jennifer took advantage of a wonderfully bright, brisk winter's day to escort Oliver about the walled village of Perth and its castle. Oliver observed that Perth differed from his own Fernwold only in detail, and, like Fernwold, Perth was growing. No longer were cottages and houses confined within the walls; now, construction had ventured to the fields beyond—and not just the stout, easily defended homes of the wealthy, but also modest cabins for a new breed, migrants human and nightcreature. Jennifer had even encountered a minotaur pair who had come to help plow the fields the preceding spring and stayed on in general service to the duchy.

They had returned to the sumptuous dinner prepared by Mrs. Creech. And dessert in the inn parlor.

They devoured their pie and custard quickly enough, and then they had only one another. "Tell me about your loss,

Oliver." Jennifer sucked at the last of the gelatinous cherry juice clinging stubbornly to her spoon.

"My loss . . ." Oliver murmured thoughtfully. "I think I'd rather not." He was silent a moment, then: "Comedy or tragedy?"

"Just a little of both, please."

Oliver talked.

He spoke of childhood warmth and happiness turned suddenly cold as a rift opened between his parents, and of the coming of Geoffrey Turner and the events following.

Jennifer listened attentively, asking only an occasional question.

"And then the bastard *died* on me," Oliver said. "He lay there and let himself die!"

"Oliver, he could hardly help it! From the sound of it, the demons and that metallic monster tore him up quite a bit."

"I guess I'm just angry—mostly at myself. I haven't a tenth his knowledge or ability."

"You still carry on Turner's work, though. You drive about in his van, saving young damsels from vampires." She stroked his arm playfully. "Grateful young damsels."

She leaned over and kissed him softly on the cheek, then the mouth.

He tensed.

"Relax, Oliver. I'm just showing you I *like* you." She leaned suddenly against his chest.

He could do nothing but put his arms around her and hold her. It was as if she were melting into him. Her hair was flower-sweet, her body vulnerable and trusting in his embrace. Soft, so very soft!

"Please, just hold me, Oliver. I don't want to talk anymore."

He patted her gently on the back and they settled into a more comfortable position. Oliver closed his eyes and his senses opened to accept the trembling creature in his embrace.

"Oh, Oliver," she said. "I feel so . . . so very strange." She looked up with fear in her eyes, and all he saw were her lips. Suddenly they were kissing once again. After a time, she nuzzled against him, her breath a hot sigh against his skin.

Don't think, Oliver told himself. Don't think. You *think* too much, and you always ruin everything. Relax. He could almost *read* Jennifer's emotions.

Suddenly her voice grew insistent: "Oliver. I *want* you."

She moved her lips lightly across his nose, down his cheek.

"Dear Jennifer," he said. "I think you already have me."

She opened her mouth and bit down hard on his throat.

The night was all star sparkle and moongleam on snow. The smell of evergreen was in the air, the clean, chill scent of winter.

Vlad Paler had transferred Hampton to his top pocket. From which vantage, the homunculus observed their progress with foreboding; he had only witnessed winter through Darkwing's senses. Actually to experience it firsthand was quite another thing.

They traveled in silence for some time and it was clear that Paler knew Hampton would not attempt escape through the snow. Nevertheless, he had not yet hinted at their destination.

As they approached a crack in the upper portion of the mountain from which mist billowed in great clouds, Paler paused to catch his breath.

"I should very much like to know what's inside there."

"Hmm? Oh, yes," Paler said. "I do owe you an explanation. You've quite an important mission ahead of you, Mr. Hampton. I presume you are by now aware of the reason this planet is the way it is."

"I live in an intelligent jabberwock."

"Of course. Well, one hundred and fifty years past, when I was in Satan's favor, my hunger for knowledge was insatiable. While exploring memory crystals I'd chanced upon in an obscure computer, I discovered that when the Second Victorian Empire discovered Styx it was *inhabited!* Some kind of alien outpost, evidently. A show of force probably persuaded them to leave, but no record of that seems to exist. I did learn, however, that the only artifact of the alien race is in this cavern. In due course, I visited it, but learned very little. You'll soon understand why. It could be quite important, though. And Hampton, you might well be the one to unlock its secrets."

"Why me?" He received no reply.

Mist enveloped them as Paler descended cautiously by the light of his electrostaff.

Gray-black splotches of fungus coated the cavern walls and glowed softly. The clicks and murmurs of bats on the walls above echoed into a cacophonic dirge. Gradually, moss-glimmer gave way to soft radiance, making it almost possible to travel without the bulb's light. The passage eventually opened into a wide chamber where a large pool bubbled gently and gave birth to wraiths of noxious mist.

Paler switched off the staff. "Well, now. We need but skirt the pool to reach our destination."

A sound echoed in the chamber.

"What's *that?*" Hampton demanded. It came again. And again.

Claws?

Twenty yards away, a head emerged from behind a quartz outcrop. Reptilian eyes transfixed them. There was a flicker of tongue as the creature tested their smell and warmth.

The creature's ears were webbed membranes, its jaws crowded with long, sharp teeth.

"You're new here, aren't you?" Paler asked, walking nonchalantly toward the creature.

"About a year," the dragon answered harshly. It emerged farther from its tunnel, revealing bright green and mottled-gray scales, and a pair of ridiculous vestigial wings. The underside of the dragon's neck and chest was horny hide. Spikes protruded above its spine.

"Mind if we have a look about?" Paler was all congeniality.

Nictitating eyelids lowered. "You're not going to fool with me treasure hole, are ya?"

"Who? *Us?*" Paler asked with an innocent expression on his face.

"Folks come around once in a while to have a look. Demons. Satyrs. Some men. You know what I do?"

Paler cleared his throat uneasily. "No. What?"

"I eat them."

"We only want to have a look. We can't very well *steal* it, can we?"

"Doesn't make any difference. I'm hungry."

The creature leaped at them.

"Christ!" a voice cried from somewhere. "What are you doing, girl!"

Something warm and loved and needed was pulled from him and Oliver grabbed for it, but it was yanked beyond reach.

His throat burned at its departure and the pain restored

his vision. He gasped for breath. Something warm and sticky had dripped down his chest.

He turned and recognized Penton struggling with someone, a blonde with disheveled, bloodstained clothing. Two blows stilled the struggling girl, and Penton hurled her against the wall, where she slumped unconscious.

"God, man!" Penton said, kneeling beside Oliver. "Are you all right?"

"What happened?"

"Isn't it obvious? Your dear Miss Eden has been at your neck. She's too far gone! I'm going to get MacPherson. And his sword."

Somehow, Oliver regained his feet. "No! You'll do nothing of the sort, Penton."

The manservant swung about. "Don't be a fool, Oliver!"

"Penton. You will tell *no one!*"

"But sir!"

"That is an order." He felt woozy. "There must be . . . another way." A flash of Jennifer's warmth, her softness came to him. "For love of me, do not, Penton!"

Oliver's legs buckled and he succumbed to the haze.

Oliver blinked. A figure before him resolved into focus. Penton's prematurely bald head gleamed in the firelight. His mustache was mussed. Oliver smelled cherry pie and burned wood.

"Jennifer!" He made to rise but was halted by Penton.

"I've put her to bed."

"She—she's *not* what you think."

"I know. She came to her senses and saw the blood. She's up there crying now."

"Does anyone else know?"

Penton shook his head solemnly.

"They mustn't learn. MacPherson will kill her." He placed a hand to his neck. No pain, no ache. He felt only two small bumps. "What do you think happened, Penton?"

The manservant stood and walked to the fire. "I don't know. The disease must be working on her. But she's alive —a sweet, charming girl! It shouldn't be doing these things to her."

"If she dies, she's gone."

"As are you, Oliver."

"Same boat. Yes. The Vampire Lord will have us, somehow. Penton, if not for this predicament, I think I'd just find a hole and crawl in."

"You've been working yourself too hard, sir. The weight of this world is not on your shoulders. You should be watching out for your*self*, if I may be so bold."

"A load off you, eh, Penton?" Oliver smiled sardonically. "Nice just to mix drinks and press slacks once again, I suppose."

"I've no objection to either task."

Oliver slouched on the divan. "Oh, Penton! What can we do?"

"You already know, don't you, sir."

Oliver peeked through his fingers. "Yes. We've two choices, haven't we? Seek out this Vampire Lord, or . . ."

"Or string along with our mystery man, MacPherson." Penton stroked his mustache back into place. "Something's strange with him. And it's not just self-delusion, either."

"Oh?"

"Today, as I worked on the van, MacPherson came to speak with me—the usual 'Prepare your soul to meet its Maker lest you be doomed to hellfire.' Well, right in the midst of 'for He is a wise and wrathful God,' the blighter just *froze*. Mouth open, eyes staring into nothing, statue-stiff. Then I heard this buzzing—quiet, mind you—coming from his head. Droned about ten seconds, then stopped. Damned if old MacPherson didn't snap right out of it and say with his best Scots burr, "I must go off alone and commune with my Creator.""

Oliver sat straight up. "A calltone! He *is* a mandroid, then!"

"Not necessarily. Could be just an implant by his ear-drum, don't you think?"

"Implanted by whom? Or what?"

"Something directs him, sir. And it *can't* be this Vampire Lord. Maybe it *is* God." He smiled grimly. "If it is, I'd better start doing some repenting."

"So you're saying there might be someplace to go for help."

"Yes, sir. But that depends entirely upon MacPherson. He's our link to this possibility—which, you must admit, seems a lesser danger than a trek for the Vampire Lord."

"My curiosity is piqued in both directions, but I'd rather not have to choose."

"My company has improved your character no end, Oliver Dolan."

"That's it, then." Oliver slapped his knees and stood. "Let's find MacPherson."

"I believe he's downstairs lecturing the locals on the evils of drink."

Oliver nodded as he walked to the window. The panes were framed in a frosty white lace. Outside, snow was settling silently to the cobbles. "You know, Penton, I'm not sure now if I'm more afraid of what's out there"—he tapped the window—"or what's in here." He tapped his temple.

Caspar Penton pointed up to the room where Jennifer Eden lay. "And what about what's up there, sir?"

Oliver sighed. "I think—I think . . . Oh God, Penton. Maybe I think too much."

"You have to decide that for yourself."

"Yes, and that's our curse, isn't it?"

"And our comfort."

Oliver glanced once more at the quiet beyond the window, shook his head slowly, and then descended into the smoke and bustle of the pub.

Paler fired the shotgun.

Even through the cloth of the pocket, Hampton could make out the muzzle flash. He ventured a look over the lip of the pocket, hands trembling.

The dragon hurtled toward them, blood and smoke pouring from its chest.

"Hell." Paler fired again. Two fountains of flesh and blood and metallic bits now spouted from the dragon's shoulder; its membranous wings were shredded.

"Damnation!" Paler cursed, then cracked open the shotgun and dug in his coat pocket for shells. The second blast had nearly disabled the dragon, but still it stumbled forward. Paler slammed two more shells into the breech.

Hampton abandoned ship. He climbed from the pocket, hung just a moment, then dropped to the ground and scrambled behind an outcrop of quartz. He turned in time to see the beast's terminal lunge.

The vampire lord let go with both barrels of the 12-gauge. The two projectiles entered the dragon's open mouth and exited just behind its webbed ears, dragging with them much of the creature's cyborg brain. Smoke mushroomed to the cave's ceiling.

"My shooting wouldn't win any prizes, Hampton, but still— Hampton?" Perplexed, he patted the pocket, then stared about the ground, neglecting for a moment the staggering dragon, which, dead, fell directly on him, pinning him to the cavern floor.

Silence.

Hampton caught up with his breathing. He could examine the artifact while Paler attempted to wiggle from beneath the dragon.

He scurried to the other side of the pool, where a mound projected from the flattened surface. Oddly angled rods projected from the mound, and they seemed to be connected by lines of a strange spangled substance. The phosphorescence of the walls was not so great in this portion of the chamber, and Hampton noticed that the mound itself pulsed with an ocher and crimson effulgence. At the mound's center a round hole approximately nine inches across radiated what felt like subsonic music.

Hampton shuddered, stared at the mound for a few moments, then scurried back to the dragon's carcass. The creature had fallen on its face and two shiny black shoes protruded, toe up, from just below its ruined chest.

Gingerly, Hampton stepped around pools of dragon blood. On the other side of the creature, Vlad Paler's head and shoulders could be seen. His hair lay like an ink stain on the ground. His eyes were closed.

Hampton could hear no breathing. "Oh, that's bloody marvelous. Here I am, stuck in this Godforsaken hole, and you're dead!" He kicked the head.

Paler's eyes sprang open. "Ouch!"

"You're alive!"

"I think so. Goodness, what happened?"

"You ass. Can't you see? The dragon fell on you."

"Ah!" Paler squirmed about, but to no avail. "Well, nothing broken. Bastard's dead, correct?"

"Yes, and he's going to lay there and rot, with you beneath him."

"That *is* a problem, isn't it? I say, you wouldn't have a go at lifting the creature off, would you, Hampton?"

"Me! How? Besides, why *should* I? I can see now what you were up to. You want me to explore the artifact. What do you think I'm going to find down there, a magic lamp with a genie inside!"

"More, perhaps," Paler replied as he tried once again to slide from beneath the expired dragon. Gasping with exertion, he stopped. "Well. I can't rely on that mangy pack of mine, can I? I do think, though, you can move the dragon off me. I'll tell you how and why.

"I believe the thing's mechanical faculties will be functional for a bit longer. Take my Swiss Army knife, crawl inside the beast, and hot-wire the mechanism. The spasm will surely roll it off me. As to *why* you should do this—neither you nor your friend Darkwing have a chance of survival without me."

Hampton considered that a moment. "Very well—a bargain. I get you out of your situation, you stick me back inside of Darkwing and let us go."

"Excellent. I'll just find another jabberwock. No problem."

"That didn't take much negotiation."

"Dear chap, I'm in no position to argue."

"Also, you tell me a little about that artifact."

"I believe it's a portal to another world. Perhaps another universe!"

"The world of those aliens you mentioned before?"

"Yes. When I first discovered it, I tried to penetrate it. Anything robotic never returned. I was developing jabberwocks at the time, and your kind to stick inside them, and I thought, *My goodness, I've stumbled upon the answer!* Homunculi! Perfect for exploring the thing, then coming back and telling me what they found!"

"You've done this before?"

"No. Didn't have time—Satan caught on to certain other of my activities. Darkwing was the first jabberwock I caught after I woke from cold sleep."

"Good enough." Hampton hopped over to Paler and tugged out the knife, which was in an elegant leather sheath. He climbed atop Vlad Paler's chest and unbuttoned the vampire's vest and shirt.

"Whatever are you doing?"

"I'm just making sure I can trust you."

The homunculus located the mandroid's chest panel, unscrewed it using the appropriate blade, and opened the small maintenance flap. Hampton selected another blade, searched for a moment, then cut deftly.

Paler was still, tense as a coiled spring.

Hampton pulled a microchip from the vampire's chest case, dropped the maintenance flap, and refastened the chest panel.

He hopped to the damp floor of the cave and smiled at Paler. "There. Now *you* need *me* if you're to return to your castle. *And* to replace this chip correctly. Only *I* can do it!"

"You little bastard! I can't see."

"Only part of its function, Paler. I'll return it when we're back and Darkwing is free."

"I don't have any choice now. Just get this monster off me."

Hampton found the nearest aperture provided by the shotgun. He squeezed through the gore and flesh and plastic to be about his job.

As it touched metal, the wire sparked.

"Now!" Hampton cried.

The behemoth jerked and rolled, then spasmed a few times before halting totally.

"Are you *out?*" Hampton asked.

"Excellent! Yes, and I'm quite well. I must admit, you *are* a most competent little bugger. Come on out."

"Right." Hampton wriggled through the dragon's carcass, heading for the glow at the shotgun hole. As he was about to exit, he had an inspiration. Slicing off a bit of dragon flesh about his own size, he pushed it through the hole ahead of him.

It immediately disappeared. "Got you, you little piece of dung."

Hampton jumped silently from the dragon's body to find Paler wrestling with the chunk of bloody flesh.

"Apparently, I *can't* trust you, Paler!" Hampton ran.

Paler was furious. Screaming and cursing, he blindly staggered about, swinging his shotgun. "You'll regret this!" Hampton did not respond. "You think you have me, do you?" Paler cried, making his way by touch to the exit. "You're wrong! I've got you. I don't need my eyes. I've other senses. In the meantime, you've two choices. You can descend into the portal or you can eat rotting dragon flesh! I will be back!" The vampire crawled away.

After a time, Hampton heard a loud explosion, and the rumble of falling rock. Paler had blocked the exit.

ACT TWO

"Blessed be the paps which Thou hast sucked."
                                    —*Luke* 11
Suppose He had been tabled at thy teats,
    Thy hunger feels not what he eats;
He'll have his teat ere long (a bloody one),
    The Mother then must suck the Son.

                        —Richard Crashaw
                          (1613–1649)

II: 1

THE SNOW that was present the first three days of the journey melted slowly. Soon the horses were splashing through streams of mud and the van's sides were caked with the stuff. But winter had only begun to loose its grasp, and patches of snow still remained from the deep drifts.

Stiff and stern upon his mount, Roald MacPherson led them through thaw, light, and dark, hatchet nose pointing west, mind intent upon the Lord's most recent assignment: find the cure for Oliver Dolan and Jennifer Eden; only *then* continue destruction of the vampires and the search for the Vampire Lord.

While Oliver and Jennifer passed the time inside the van, Oliver introduced her to Geoffrey Turner's music crystals. Rock she thought interesting but not terribly exciting. She preferred romantic classical pieces and folk music. Often as not, Oliver would bow to her preferences, restricting his rock music to the headphones. This pleased Penton and MacPherson no end.

No, to Oliver the travel was not at all boring, the rattle of the van wheels and the squeak of its axles hardly monotonous. The ennui induced by the wintry countryside was soon overcome by the moment-to-moment adventure of discovering Jennifer. She moved him where he thought all feelings had been bolted down solid.

One night, they had ended the day with gentle talk and Jennifer had fallen asleep beside him. Oliver lay awake, staring intently at the campfire. *What a wonderful person she is,* he thought, and the images and impressions of the day streamed through his mind like the memory of a lovely song.

He had never felt about anyone the way he felt about Jennifer Eden. She was beautiful, unpredictable, wonderful. . . .

And Jennifer Eden, still asleep, rolled slightly toward him as if to touch him, murmuring softly, "I feel the same way."

The sun was spreading shadows through the forest, when highwaymen wielding a motley assortment of guns and crossbows stepped from the sunset. They were six, evenly divided between men and trolls.

"Your money or your lives!" a troll cried in a gravelly voice. He waved a single-shot pistol before MacPherson.

MacPherson's steed bucked and whinnied, but he held it firm. "Good afternoon," he said, signaling Oliver to halt the van. "I'm afraid our pounds number not many more than our lives."

"We'll take whatever you got." The man was squat, his ugly face pitted with scars. "Horses look nice. Maybe we'll have those as well. You can walk to Bridgeport."

Trolls were a curiously stupid lot, not commonly encountered. Of identical height, weight, and appearance—perhaps three hundred pounds each, measuring exactly six feet —they were porcine brutes with snouts, elephantlike ears, and a mass of wiry hair. All manner of debris, dust, leaves, burrs, and more noisome things tended to collect in their steely crowns, which seldom were washed for fear of rust. Their teeth were incredibly large and sharp.

The trolls awkwardly gripped their pistols, sneering and salivating stupidly, obviously hopeful that their intended victims would give opposition so as to visit violence upon them.

Well, Oliver Dolan thought, raising his hands high to show he carried no weapons, *at least the humans in the company could be reasoned with.*

"Don't worry," he whispered to Jennifer beside him on the front seat of the van. "We can spare the money."

"Yes," Jennifer said. "But we can't spare our lives!"

"What's happening?" Penton poked his head from the van's open door, and immediately grasped the situation. "Ah. Brigands!"

"Penton!" Oliver called. "Gather our money. Bring it out!"

"Right, sir."

The man, who seemed to serve as leader, stepped forward. "And any valuables as well!"

"Oh, and Penton!" Oliver said. "Do bring out those nice *jewel* boxes for the gentlemen, won't you?"

MacPherson was still, but managed to keep his hand near his sword without causing undue alarm in the robbers. The squat, unkempt leader stumbled forward to point at the van's ill-lit interior. A swarthy man, his coat was covered with patches. "See that the fellow doesn't take too long, or we'll plug one of ya just for practice, hear?"

"I say, Mr. Highwayman. Business not been good this winter?" Oliver asked. "You look a bit worn."

"We be thieves now, young son, but only because we be in need. Crack mercenary team, we are, and soon we be 'irin' ourselves out to the 'ighest bidder."

"What? You anticipate war hereabouts?"

"Spoilin' for a fight, down south, the Amalgamation 'n the Holy States. Got their noses up each other's arses, they do, 'n there's goin' to be some sneezin' soon, har har."

Jennifer whispered, "I wonder what our Vampire Lord friend has to do with *that*."

"What d'you say, tart?"

"I'm nothing of the sort!" Jennifer cried.

At that moment, Penton exited the van, ceremoniously holding out a stack of lead boxes topped by a small pouch. The pile tottered and the sheer bulk of the booty made the thieves' eyes bulge.

"C'mon, c'mon," the leader called, motioning with his free hand. "Over here, quickly."

Penton managed to tote the pile to the highwayman, and placed the small treasure trove before him. The other bandits moved around him.

The rogue in charge immediately hoisted the purse, undid the strings. A small pile of coins fell into his hand. His smile turned into a scowl. "What the 'ell is this? A noble company like yours, traveling so poorly? I don't believe it for a moment. What's 'ere? Maybe ten bleedin' crowns 'n a few shillin's? C'mon, let's have the stuff you got strapped 'round your waist. Those duds you're wearing mean you got more coins than *this!*"

"Please," Penton said, bowing curtly in a gesture of perfect servitude. "We have thus far carried our wealth in more concrete terms." He eyed the stacked lead boxes significantly.

The leader paused a moment, then held up a hand covered by a glove with its fingers snipped off. The fingers twiddled and his eyes glittered with delight.

The others of his band kept their weapons trained but with noticeably less interest than before as they rummaged through the stack to glimpse their prizes. The trolls creaked and shuddered, but their enthusiasm overpowered their physical limitations.

"What's in it, Master Jerkin?" one asked with childlike wonder. "Hurry and open it."

Master Jerkin did just that, holding it under their noses.

Oliver tensed. If there were going to be a fight, this was its moment.

The box opened, revealing a radioactive cross nestled in velvet. The nearest troll managed a brief bug-eyed stare, then extended a hairy paw to pick up the object. It was gone in a single gulp. He smacked his lips and leered. The other two trolls grabbed boxes, opened them, and ate the contents.

Eyes wide with consternation, Master Jerkin opened and closed his mouth like a fish out of water. "What—what are you bastards *doing?*" The trolls were already reaching for seconds, but Master Jerkin yanked the remaining boxes out of reach. "What *are* these things?"

"Candy crosses, yes, yes," one of the trolls said, rubbing his belly with pleasure. "Satan gave us these for Lucifer-mass, he did! Delicious, those were. But these are a little stale."

"You *idiots!*" Master Jerkin opened another of the boxes and tapped a cross. "Jewelry. *Metal!* Not candy! You just ate your share of the booty!"

"That's all right," the nearest troll said. He belched re-soundingly.

Master Jerkin spun to face Penton. "Right. What else have you got tucked away in there. I want it *all!*"

"I assure you, sir, nothing else is of value."

"Let's have a look. Lads! Keep your guns ready, and don't hesitate to plug 'em. I—" He turned to a troll. " 'ere, Swamp. What's wrong with you! I said, keep the gun *up!*"

The troll had bent over and turned an astonishing shade of purple. "Tummy ache!" he rumbled.

"Cripes! Serve you right for eating—"

The other two suddenly doubled over, groaning as well. Master Jerkin and his human cohorts gaped at this display, lowering their weapons.

Oliver immediately launched himself at the nearest, landing squarely on the thief's back, propelling the man into the mud. The fellow jerked around with his pistol, firing without a target, but mud had clogged the barrel and the weapon exploded in his hand. He screamed.

The other man swung his crossbow around to finish Oliver, but Jennifer hurled herself upon him as he triggered the bow, and the quarrel pierced Master Jerkin's left foot. That worthy, until then attempting to bring his own weapon to bear, stared down quietly for a moment, and then began to scream.

Caspar Penton stepped from the rear of the van, holding a cocked rifle. "Something of value I neglected. Now all of you, be very, very still."

The trolls, detecting a fracas, tried to stand and attend to their favorite pastime. With a *flick!* Roald MacPherson's sword blazed alight. Thrice it descended.

Just then, Jennifer picked herself up from the mud. "I'm all *dirty!*"

"Get *away* from the——"

The brigand she had attacked reached beneath his coat and extracted a pistol. Leaning over quickly, he grabbed Jennifer, obviously hoping to make his escape with her as shield. But Penton fired and the bullet caught the man squarely in the throat. Clutching Jennifer, he staggered while blood pumped from his jugular, then fell on the girl, pinning her to the ground. Oliver feared that she'd been hurt. He ran to Jennifer and pushed the dead thief off her, into the mud.

Jennifer lay covered with mud. The dead man had painted her neck and her face bright red. Her eyes were open to the sky.

Oliver leaned over her. "Jenny, are you all right?"

Her eyes found his, but her expression did not change. Blood filled her mouth.

She nodded.

Then swallowed.

II: 2

"MARVELOUS STUFF, WINE," Vlad Paler said, holding a goblet to the light. It sparkled red in his grasp. Suddenly, he grimaced and downed the entire glass. A small stream slipped down his chin and onto his chest, where it was absorbed by a linen gown. "Must it be so painful, Mendelsohn?"

The sweating doctor peered up through thick glasses that magnified his flinty eyes absurdly. "It cannot be less so, your grace. After all, you must direct the operation."

"My first direction is to Meredith, yonder." He beckoned at a shapely young woman occupying a chaise by the computer console. "More wine, Meredith."

She quickly carried a silver decanter to Paler's cup. Paler smiled at her. "Dr. Mendelsohn, are you certain a transfusion is not necessary?" Paler lowered his glass, then gently stroked the girl's neck. "A gentleman occasionally thinks of things other than wine."

Mendelsohn slipped off his scanner. "I cannot diagnose properly while you joke. I need your assistance, Paler. Kindly remember: before entering your employ, I was a mere surgeon, a cutter of flesh with some electronics background."

"You have come far with me, and I am well pleased. Now, what the hell is *wrong* with me!"

"Restoring the microchip you lost was simplicity itself," the doctor murmured. "As for what's wrong now . . . well, at least you've something similar back."

"A neatly executed job. It was a shame I had to cannibalize one of my best servants for the part—but then I demand only the best."

"He gave his eyesight gladly for you, my Lord," an attendant offered from the shadows.

"Bloody sycophant! He knows it's covered by the house policy. He's sacrificed nothing!"

"Yes, my Lord."

Mendelsohn refitted the scanner. Paler's rib cage lay open before his pillowed head. Within the chest cavity, in folds of veined and arteried flesh, lay layers of microcircuitry pulsing with electric life. The diagnostic scanner was connected to a mobile unit that projected a hologram of Paler's circuitry. As the scanner's probe moved, the hologram did also, the scanner's central processing unit adding graphic symbols to represent subsystem status.

Paler stared at the representation while Mendelsohn scanned, occasionally stopping to examine another level of circuitry. "Not simple, this," the doctor murmured. "Satan's best work."

"Satan's! I'll have you know that the most brilliant circuitry was designed by me!"

"A self-made vampire?"

"I make the jokes around here, Doctor!"

The doctor shrugged. "One of the hazards of having a human assistant. Has a mind of his own, Paler."

Vlad Paler was not listening. "I say, do that again!"

"Pardon?"

"Run the bleeder over the braincase binary line. Bit of an irregularity there, I think."

Mendelsohn obeyed, and a dotted line raced over the corresponding section of the schematic. "What do you think, Doctor? Too much resistance? Maybe that's why I get the infernal headaches, the wretched dreams."

Mendelsohn turned to a technician. "Run an analysis." The response was immediate, but the doctor had to squint to make out the finer symbols. "No. Matches previous readings perfectly."

"What did the little bugger *do* to me, then?"

"It's really quite simple. I'll call up the previous schematics and we'll compare."

Several diagrams materialized. Mendelsohn aligned them, then focused upon the section that held the suspect microchip. "Now, look here. It's obvious if you *want* to see it, Paler. That component of yours, though similar to many others, was unique. More complex, for one thing. My guess is that it processed more than just video data. Off hand, I would say its removal has somehow rendered you vulnerable to radio waves at certain frequencies or, perhaps, certain types of rf modulation. You may well be reacting to solar flares. We'll have to perform further diagnostic tests so we can determine how to dampen the—er, difficulty."

"That little *bastard!* Well, he'll pay when he gets back. I can get by. The world will just be a little nastier with my headaches." He waved his hand. "Now, stuff me back together quickly, Mendelsohn. There are things to do."

The assistant nodded and hurriedly reassembled and sealed Paler's chest. As Mendelsohn was closing the top of his tool caddy, a voice blasted from an unseen loudspeaker, causing the doctor and Paler to jump with alarm. "Lord Paler. Most urgent. A servant has—"

Paler hit a button and screamed into a nearby microphone, "For God's sake, not so loud."

"Sorry, my Lord. But the survivor of that routed den has arrived."

Paler blinked. "Gracious me. Well, send him in. I've been waiting for his report. The telepathy machine has been getting a muddled homing-in." He turned to the doctor. "Something we must look at later. So much to do! So much to *do!*"

Presently, the vampire arrived and was admitted. Mendelsohn wrinkled his nose at the man's stench. The middle-aged former human was a wretched sight, clothes tattered and worn, eyes sunken.

"I watched them, master. I know which way they went. I knew you'd want me to."

"Excellent. Excellent, dear chap. Let me get you a glass of wine! You tell us your story, and then you can get cleaned up. I've a tasty little village girl waiting for supper with you!" Paler nudged the bedraggled man conspiratorially.

"You're very kind." The vampire accepted the wine.

"Oh, and friend. Could you stand on the other side of the room? No offense, but you're a bit ripe."

"Yes, master." The vampire shuffled back and began his story.

Vlad Paler became progressively more upset, particularly about the stern fellow with the fiery sword. By the time the vampire had finished his tale, Paler was pacing furiously. "This . . . this portends no good. Come, Mendelsohn. Immediate measures must be taken."

As they left the chamber, Vlad Paler thought of something. "I say, I've quite forgotten your name, friend."

"It's Eden, sir. Fredrick Eden."

II: 3

>■<■-0-■■-0-■■-0-■■-0-■■-0-■■<

Darkwing had always hated oceans.

He hated the briny smell of the coast, the stench of rotting fish, the scent of drying seaweed. Most of all, he hated the sea beasties. They were *bigger* than he, and always hungry.

During the previous hundred years or so, Satan had begun to replace many of his seathings with creatures totally biological. Though not totally in the creator's power, nonetheless they were as efficient at destroying ships and terrorizing the seacoast as any of the radio-controlled sort—and reproduced themselves as well! Satan maintained enough of the cyborgs to police the natural monsters and see that no one species became dominant over the ocean, but *all* the living things he'd introduced were so fearsome that the system generally remained stable.

Nonetheless, there Darkwing stood, on a creaking pier, watching seagulls and waiting to board the channel ferry piloted by a standard model, i.e., nasty, Neptune. While untangling seaweed from one of several propellers with the barbed ends of his trident, this one was expounding at length upon the faults of liberated nightcreatures, jabberwocks in particular.

The Neptune unleashed a particularly obscene volley as he jerked at tendrils of vegetation below the waterline, then hurled a clump of the smelly stuff at Darkwing. "Fancy this crap? Oh, yes—all I got on board for chow is salt pork and biscuits, and that's *not* included in the fare."

"My guv'nor will take up the slack, I'm sure." Darkwing felt queasy as he unwrapped a strand of seaweed from his long neck.

"Fancy-pants bugger, that Mr. Vlad M. Paler."

"*Lord* Paler, to you."

"Yeah, well, he pays good. Can't fault him that. Even enough to haul a jabberwock, as disgusted as your sort makes me."

"I think I can live without further conversation."

"Well, it comes with the trip. Take it or leave it." The Neptune rubbed his protuberant green belly and chortled merrily. He was an odd-looking fish, what with fins on shins and forearms for easy swimming. But well designed enough, Darkwing thought. Whatever else one could say about Satan, it took a touch of genius to devise a world as truly warped as this.

"I have no choice." Darkwing reluctantly boarded the ship, repairing to a clear area above the machinery spaces, where he curled up into a tight ball and silently watched Neptune prepare to cast off.

Abruptly, a mechanism imbedded in Darkwing's chest crackled to life, causing no end of electrical discomfort. "Prepare for—*click!*—short wave—*click! click!*—message with graphics."

Cursing quietly, Darkwing rose on his haunches to allow the screen/lens a clear view of the ferry. "Am I coming through, jabberwock?"

"Too well."

"Yes. I see Neptune 34 yonder. Give him my very best."

"What do you want?" the jabberwock growled. "I'm following directions. When are you going to tell me what you've done with Hampton?"

"In good time. Right now, I've some directions for you. When you cross I want you to head west, instead of east, to Carraway, and from there toward Blitherton."

Darkwing did a double take, then bent his head toward the monitor in his chest so that he was able to stare at the image of Vlad Paler, albeit upside down. *"What? That will take me through some of the worst nightcreature territory on the continent!"*

"Precisely. Which will allow me to chat with their leaders, if it doesn't take too much time. Your priority is to find Oliver Dolan and the firesword-bearing chap, after all."

"Yes," Darkwing said. Staring at Paler's inverted image was dizzying him. He retracted his neck. "And then I get Hampton back?"

"Absolutely. Ta ta for now. I'll be in touch."

The picture fizzled into blankness.

The great engines of the vessel thrummed to life under Neptune's ministrations and the ferry moved slowly out to sea. Course set, Neptune leaned over the railing of the control deck and looked down to where Darkwing huddled uneasily on the main deck.

"Been workin' this sea for nigh on two centuries, I have." He took a big gulp of the sea air. The wind blew back his curly pea-green locks as the boat churned through the swells. "Things used to be much calmer when orders came from Central. 'S why I like workin' for your Mr. Paler. Gotta have some order to this world, I say, and Mr. Paler seems a worthwhile enough bloke. Pays damned decent, I'll give him that. No, from what I hear, things are disorganized all over. Just ain't natural, nightcreatures hookin' up with armies of real men. Don't like it. Don't like it one bit. 'Tain't no good goin' to come of it, I can tell you that. That's one of the reasons I'm ferryin' you across. *Only* reason I'd ferry a damned jabberwock. Last time I dealt with one of your ilk, he shortchanged me on the fare. You things were never quite right, even when old Nick was calling the shots. You always had larcenous thoughts, even then." He pulled out a stick of chewing tobacco previously wedged into his discolored leather belt. "But I tell you one thing, Jabberwock. This stretch of sea is *mine*. I call the shots here. The beasties 'round about, they hear my engines, they take notice and they run if I tell 'em to run, and they come if I tell 'em to come." He confidently patted a tarnished computer panel beside him. "They know who's boss around here, they do!"

Darkwing groaned to himself as Neptune's self-important monologue continued. He lay for a while and tried to sleep, but that was impossible.

Without warning, Darkwing felt his gorge rising. He lifted his woozy body and dragged himself to the railing and threw up voluminously into the water, to Neptune's laughter. "Damn me, if you ain't a sight." The giant roared with laughter.

A patch of water ahead began to boil furiously. Suddenly a huge tentacle burst from the depths and writhed languidly in the air. Instinctively, Darkwing backed away from the rail.

With a thunderous roar, a monstrous head reared up and purple eyes glared malevolently at the ferry. Water fountained here and there as a series of livid, sucker-covered tentacles burst from the sea. Two suddenly plucked the communications antennae.

Darkwing staggered about the deck looking for a place to hide.

Even above the ruckus of the ruinous tentacles, Darkwing could clearly hear the captain's succinct appraisal of the situation. "Oh, Hell!"

Darkwing frantically pushed at the buttons on his chest.

THOUGH THEY WERE no longer any more dangerous than days, Oliver never really grew used to being in the open during the nights. When they sat outdoors like this, even with the roaring warmth of the campfire he felt dangerously exposed.

Dishes rattled as Jennifer gathered them for cleaning. Leftover stew and steamy tea provided an aromatic memory of the quiet repast. Jennifer had said absolutely nothing as they ate, and her expression had been odd. Oliver knew he'd have to talk to her later.

The two brigands sat, securely tied, on the opposite side of the campfire, stolidly still. Jerkin occasionally growled to himself, but that was all.

Meanwhile, MacPherson sat upon a rock, sipping tea and munching on a muffin while he decided what was to be done with them. "I would that God's voice direct me in the matter," he said finally. "In my fury I'd as soon execute these scum. But mercy compels me to free them. However, should they be punished before then? If so, what shall that punishment be?" Setting down his mug, he clasped his hands and directed his eyes upward. "Anoint my head with Thy precious words, O Lord!"

"Oh, bloody Hell," Jerkin said. "You've tortured us enough already! We didn't want to hurt nobody."

"God has not spoken to me yet," the grim man returned. "I await His word on the matter."

"You've got all night." Penton ambled off to join Jennifer in washing the dishes.

"You and your stupid ideas!" Thompson muttered. "Join up with those imbecilic trolls on some half-baked mercenary venture. I should never have let you talk me into it. I should have hired myself out for manual labor to those dimwitted twerps at HOPE. At least they're harmless!"

"Look. I'm the one with the hole in my foot. You're right as rain."

"And the way it's going, I'll be inside a dungeon or something, right as rain. And poor Edwards—"

With a suddenness that startled Thompson, Oliver leaped

up and grasped the man by his frayed collar. "What did you say? Where were you offered employment?"

"God, don't hurt 'im!" the man on the ground said. "We're just talking 'bout someplace we passed two weeks ago!"

"But you said 'HOPE.' You said *'HOPE.' The Holy Order to Preserve the Empire!*"

"Yeah! That's what they called themselves," the man managed to spit out. "Loony as they come, though I've seen some plenty strange places in my travels."

"And you say it's only two weeks away! Penton! Did you *hear* that? HOPE! We've found it! While we weren't looking for it, we found it!" Oliver turned back to Thompson. "It's a castle, isn't it? It's a castle with only a small community within."

"Why, yes. But what the devil you getting so upset for?"

"You can *take* us there? You can trace your way *back!*" Oliver shook the man with violent enthusiasm.

Penton stepped up and placed a restraining arm on his master. "I don't think that's necessary, sir."

"We can do that—but you got to promise. We take you there, you let us go. Maybe give us a coin or two."

"Absolutely."

Oliver was beside himself with joy. Jennifer approached warily. He grabbed her by the arm. "HOPE, Jenny. Finally, HOPE!"

Jennifer just stared at him.

Oliver turned impatiently to MacPherson. "Mr. MacPherson. HOPE is the organization that Geoffrey Turner established. You've certainly heard of it before, haven't you? Is that where you're *from,* perhaps?"

"HOPE?" the gaunt man whispered. "HOPE." He looked up. "Please, excuse me. I must seek solitude to pray for knowledge and guidance." Roald MacPherson strode into the darkness.

Turning to Penton, Oliver said, "Well, something definitely troubles him about it. There's no question, though, that this is where we have to go first, no matter what he decides. If Turner's Holy Order is still intact, it might be capable of preventing the impending chaos."

"And that is more important than the—um, health of you and Jennifer?" Penton asked.

"With HOPE, Penton, we are dealing with a known quantity. Perhaps they even have a cure for the disease. After all, they know something of science. What do we know of MacPherson except that he's off his head and thinks he receives orders from God? No, I think there's a better chance for a cure at HOPE headquarters."

"I must confess, the notion of finding HOPE rather intrigues me."

"Excellent. I shall discuss it with Jenny as well. She should have a voice in the matter, I think."

"Or should be allowed to think so," Penton commented wryly.

"It's that sort of attitude, Penton, that has gotten males in trouble for centuries."

"It's that sort of attitude, sir, that has *kept* us male for *millennia*."

Jenny had returned to cleaning up, a task she did not relish. But it was her turn for the job. Oliver went to help her.

She sat under a battery-powered fluorescent lamp attached to the van. She had washed off the worst of the mud and the blood and changed clothes, but winter travels did not allow for spring-side bathing, nor make laundering an attractive chore. The freshness of Jennifer's attire had suffered.

Her hair had dried in tangled clumps and the rigors of the journey had not done wonders for her complexion. Jennifer was out of her normal environment and not prepared to accept the dues extracted by the journey.

She did not look at Oliver. "God! I *hate* doing dishes. My hands become dry and the skin cracks. I just *hate* it."

"I'd help you wash, but—" He held up his bandaged hand.

"Dry, then."

"I'll dry."

They finished the task in silence, then stored the dinnerware in the van.

"I'm sorry that all this has to happen to someone like you," Oliver said as they closed the china cabinet.

"And you're not sorry it's happening to you?"

"It *is* frightening."

"It makes me feel very fragile, Oliver. I felt so secure at home."

"That was a lie, Jennifer. If I've learned anything lately, it's that there's no such thing as security."

"But it's such a lovely illusion." She looked at him. "I feel safe with you, Oliver. I do."

He looked away. "You shouldn't."

"Perhaps it's *me* you shouldn't feel safe around, after that business by the fire."

"You couldn't help yourself. Bloody business this, no?" He sighed. "Jenny, I care for you very much. Very much indeed. I'd—I'd do almost anything for you." He gently turned her head and tilted it up to face him. "Jenny!"

Tears ran down her cheeks and she was biting her lip so hard that blood had begun to well up around her incisors.

"Oh, Oliver!" She sprung up, clasped her arms around his neck, and kissed him passionately. His surprise soon melted into response.

The taste of her blood in his mouth was sweet.

She pulled back slightly away from him and smiled. "Don't be frightened. Accept." But when he made to embrace her again, she pulled away. "I look forward to seeing this HOPE place."

"Jenny. I—"

He stepped toward her, but was interrupted as MacPherson materialized in the van's entranceway. His hat was off and his locks were disheveled. His face bore the wild-eyed look of revelation. His hands were clenched.

"The Lord God has spoken!"

Somewhere, relays clicked . . .
neurotransistors emitted modulated energy . . .
lights glowed soft in darkness . . .
a tuner twirled . . . searching . . .
broadcast . . .

Slim, delicate, lithe, she moaned Vlad Paler's name in his ear, overcoming the worst of his anxieties. The spider-silk touch of her fingers wiped away images of his misadventure. He should have been more on his guard, he thought idly to the music of the young girl's sighs.

Something tingled in Paler's chest.

Puzzled, he lifted his fangs from the soft ivory throat. A minuscule drop of blood fell onto the satin sheets.

"No!" the girl pleaded. "Don't go!"

Paler rose from the bed. Weaving back and forth, eyes unfocused, he gripped his chest. "I—I feel . . . unwell." He staggered toward the door. "Call Dr. Mendel—" He pitched forward abruptly, falling to the floor.

The girl jerked up from the bed, dark tresses swirling in the candlelight. But her recent donation had left her quite weak, and she swooned onto the rug.

THE DAYS PASSED and seemed to Oliver so similar that they blurred one into another as if, after night's encampment, the party would rise and repeat the previous day instead of forging into the next.

They plodded across a muddy land, and rain fell occasionally or snow flurried. But all seemed the same. Of the nightcreatures they passed none posed a danger, not even the basilisk they'd found stooped over the body of a horse. It just eyed them warily and proceeded to eat.

MacPherson kept to himself, insisting only upon reading from his Bible before each meal and intoning and petitioning the Lord for guidance. Jerkin and Thompson spoke only to each other, except when they were giving directions.

While packing up one morning a week into their travel toward HOPE, Oliver noticed that Jenny was awfully long in returning from her toilet. Worry conquered his natural shyness and reserve. He went to see that all was well.

It took Oliver only a few moments to find Jenny.

She lay on the ground, behind a large boulder, limp, hair sprayed against wet rock. Her hands clutched at empty air like frozen claws. Her face was pale as that of a drowned woman.

A numb fear suffused Oliver.

He kneeled, then pulled her up to a sitting position.

"Jenny!" he said, shaking her. She was still warm. He could feel the rasp of difficult breaths.

Her eyelids fluttered. Suddenly she was Jenny again, eyes looking trustingly up. "I . . . I . . . feel . . ."

"Quiet. I'm going to take you back. Penton will know what to do."

"Yes. Yes, Oliver, of course." She tried to get up, could not. "This . . . this has happened to me before."

"Why didn't you tell someone?"

"MacPherson will kill me. *He* knows."

"Knows what, Jennifer?"

Her eyes went to his bandaged hand.

"Oliver," she said in a faint whisper. "Your bandage is loose. Let me tighten it."

Feebly, she began to unwrap the gauze.

Oliver's throat went dry. He did not pull away his hand. "Jenny. You mustn't."

". . . fix your bandage . . ."

"That's not what I mean. You must resist."

Silently, she finished removing the bandage. The wound was yet livid and was slow to form a scab.

Jennifer did not reply. She held the hand, staring at it. "No, Oliver. You misunderstand," she said finally. She gazed up at him with helpless eyes. "I need it, but I shall not steal it. It does not control me, though should I die, it would. Therefore, I must not die." She swallowed. "You must give it to me. Can't you see? That is where you and I are going. You're my only hope."

"I . . . I cannot."

"Dear Oliver, you are such a hypocrite. You want mine too, don't you?"

"Our relationship must be more than that, Jennifer."

"I see." She closed her eyes, seeming to faint away again. She grew limp in Oliver's embrace.

He eased her to the ground, knowing that he had a choice. He knew enough of the disease to know what she needed. He could not bear to see her die, nor could he bear the thought of her using another to fulfill her needs.

Taking a penknife from his pocket, he worried gently at his wound. It smarted, but the cupped palm slowly filled with blood.

Carefully, Oliver lifted Jennifer and placed his hand to her lips.

Her eyes flashed open, alive as Oliver had never seen them before. She licked at his offering and sighed with gratification, then kissed the wound clean and rewrapped the bandages.

After a moment more, Jennifer stood and brushed off her clothing. She hugged Oliver's arm. Her color had returned. She seemed excited and fulfilled.

As they returned to the van, Oliver was quiet and thoughtful, for the image of Jennifer's leisurely ingestion of his blood lingered in his mind's eye.

When they returned, Penton greeted them, explaining that all was ready for departure. He stared a moment at Jennifer's possessive hold on Oliver's arm. Then he looked at Oliver, smiling pleasantly.

Jenny's own smile turned brittle and cool.

Her fingers tightened around Oliver's arm.

"That's it," Jerkin said, poking a stumpy finger over the tops of the trees on the horizon. "That's the bloody place, finally. Ain't it, Thompson?"

"Sure as I live and breathe."

Above the horizon, Oliver could make out the towers of a castle. He was glad to see them, and glad that here was a place where finally they could rest and he might even obtain some privacy. Jennifer, healthy and happy under Oliver's occasional clandestine ministrations of blood—only a sip here, a slurp there, no harm at all, Oliver rationalized—had become quite exasperating, following him about, constructing elaborate futures for them once "this wearisome business is over." Despite the joys of Jennifer's company, the furtive kisses, hugs, and fond words, he craved the joys of solitude. Oliver feared to raise the subject, for he had learned rapidly that Jenny did not wish to hear the truth when it displeased her.

"You two will have your freedom," Penton said, "as soon as we determine that this is indeed our true destination."

"Aye," Roald MacPherson agreed. "And if it be not, God have pity on you." He patted the hilt of his laser sword.

Jerkin's head seemed to sink between his shoulders. "I don't like that much."

"Nor I," Thompson agreed with a frown.

Penton raised his eyebrows coolly. "Gentlemen, is there good reason for you not to meet the denizens of yon community? Some earlier indiscretion?"

Jerkin shuffled from foot to foot, uneasily eying the spires above the woods. "Well, truth to tell, we don't much like the occupants."

Thompson shook his head disgustedly. "Yeah, and we copped some silverware, too!"

"Alf!"

"Here! They know our like, Jerkin. Why not tell them the truth!"

Roald MacPherson dismounted from his mare, and strode purposefully to the two brigands, who averted their eyes. "So! Another debt. One, at least, that you can pay!"

MacPherson patted at Jerkin's scruffy blouse. Suddenly his fingers dived into the shirtfront, extricating a pouch attached to a leather thong around the man's unclean neck.

"Here! That's the last of my——"

"You will repay your debts!" MacPherson cried. He cut the pouch away and placed it in Jerkin's hands. "You will accompany us to the castle; you will confront your victims; you will prostrate yourself before them. And you *will* repay them. Then and only then will you and your companion be permitted to depart!"

Penton grinned. "I think that would be splendid."

"What? *All* of it? There's eight guineas here!"

"Yeah," Thompson added. "The silverware we nicked weren't worth half that!"

"Your victims will decide how much it was worth," MacPherson said, punctuating his statement with a clenched fist waved below Thompson's nose.

"Right!" Thompson said.

On the castle's outskirts were fields bearing the withered husks of cornstalks. The party traipsed past these toward the battlements. The castle was uncharacteristically small and no new buildings had spilled beyond the fortifications. Indeed, as they neared the place, it became obvious that the building was not well tended. Cracks were apparent in the stone walls and the parapets were badly weathered, showing no signs of recent maintenance. If not for the various signs of habitation—notably laundry hanging to dry—Oliver would have thought it long deserted.

Thompson and Jerkin sullenly led the ragtag procession. MacPherson followed erect and purposeful, eyes steadfastly focused upon the brigands, resolved to see justice done. Oliver sat between Jennifer and Penton on the van's front bench. So far the two broad, stocky horses acquired in Perth had proved reliable, and there had been no need to utilize the van's ability for self-propulsion under battery power. Though the horse-drawn mode reduced speed, it also reduced wear and tear upon the irreplaceable drive train.

Oliver's thoughts were heavy with brooding. He'd always viewed the discovery of HOPE headquarters as a thing to be desired beyond all other occurrences; an event that would lead to the further enlightenment of mankind on Styx, with his aid. It certainly seemed a worthwhile enough goal in the year and a half since the successful completion of Geoffrey Turner's quest. Now, however, with that goal in sight, its actual shape was suspect. *This* was HOPE

93

headquarters? Certainly Oliver had expected something less shabby.

Most certainly he did not expect the two basilisks that streaked through the gates, producing the most unnerving shrieks.

Basilisks were not particularly large creatures. Their bodies consisted of the rear quarters—complete with snake-like tail—of a very large lizard and the forequarters of a gigantic rooster, with talons as sharp as any sword. What basilisks lacked in size, however, they made up in fearsomeness. Of all the liberated nightcreatures, they seemed to be least equipped with potential for intelligence.

"Jenny, get down in the van," Oliver ordered.

Jennifer obeyed without objection.

The two beasts were almost upon them when Jerkin and Thompson decided to bolt.

Before they had been kept in tow by the threat of pistols. With the advent of HOPE headquarters, vigilance was relaxed somewhat. And as the basilisks bore down upon the party, even that scrutiny evaporated.

As it happened, their sprint attracted the basilisks' attention and the beasts veered toward the brigands.

"Right!" Penton said calmly. "Fire while they're close, Oliver!"

So saying, he hoisted and aimed his own weapon. With a sharp report, the rifle bucked. Blood splashed from the tail of a basilisk. The basilisk, hardly fazed, dashed determinedly toward the fleeing men, squawking ferociously.

Oliver fired and missed.

Aiming once more, Penton said, "Jennifer. Up with the electroprods, lass. We may find ourselves in need of them." He squeezed off another round. A scale blew from the basilisk's chest.

MacPherson jammed his boot heels into his mount's side and pursued the basilisks, his bright sword raised high.

Jennifer handed up two electroprods. Oliver grabbed them and handed one to Penton, who shrugged the contraption on quickly. "We'll not affect anything at this distance."

He whipped the horses, but they reared and would not advance.

Oliver hopped from the van, and Penton followed, grunting as his feet struck the ground. Together, they tore toward the imminent melee.

One of the basilisks was slightly ahead of the other and gaining on the horse bearing Thompson. Its beak lashed forward, tearing a gash in the horse's rump. The animal screamed, and bucked, throwing Thompson high into the air, then collided with Jerkin's horse, knocking him from his perch.

With an agonized howl, Jerkin fell on his back, rolled to his feet, and ran for his life.

The frontmost basilisk paused briefly over Thompson, then its beak descended to lift him off the ground and toss him as a dog tosses a bone. Thompson spun and hit the ground hard. The basilisk's claws then shredded the man.

The second basilisk paused long enough for a bit of impromptu exploratory surgery on the dead man, then struck out for Jerkin, who had managed to gain a healthy head start though his tied hands did not permit the balance necessary for a breakneck life-or-death run. He staggered a bit, but managed to retain his footing.

MacPherson galloped past Thompson, who was beyond help and recognition.

The basilisk pursuing Jerkin struck with its sharp beak, coxcomb flapping with its movement. The blow would have cracked open Jerkin's skull, had the man not dodged, skewing his path. The basilisk, not so fast on the uptake, overshot its mark and lost ground.

MacPherson thundered up close enough for an attack. His laser sword swung gracefully, on the downward arc lopping off a yard of lizard tail, which thrashed like a decapitated snake. The basilisk squawked, wheeled upon its attacker, and swung a claw. MacPherson's left arm was cut, but he did not cry out.

He arced his rapier once again, cleanly hacking off the beast's head, which rolled smoking to the ground.

MacPherson next turned his attention to the feeding basilisk, who seemed not to have noticed its companion's demise.

A shrill whistle split the air.

Immediately, the basilisk hovering over Thompson's carcass reared its head and answered with a loud crow, turned, then scampered back through the open gate, past the reach of MacPherson's laser sword or the electroprods so uselessly carried by Oliver and Penton.

A man wearing a silver chain with a tin whistle attached emerged from the gate. In one hand he held a long-stemmed glass from which he sipped daintily, occasionally venturing a glance at his harried visitors.

"I say, I *am* sorry," he finally drawled. "Beasties were a

tad overenthusiastic, I fear." He smiled, displaying a set of large, pearl-white teeth. "But do come in! We've plenty of champagne!"

"Once again, I cannot adequately express my sorrow for this wretched misfortune," Sparrow declared as he delicately poured a second round of champagne for his visitors. "The basilisks were supposed to detain guests, not digest them. I trust that you are not in too much distress, sirrah. Surely, just a sip of this tonic will ease the smart, yes?"

"I told you, I do not partake of alcoholic beverages," MacPherson stated stonily. His left arm rode in a sling. "My calling forbids it."

"But surely even Christ himself tippled, gentle sir!" The man was thin, dapper, poised elegantly. "And, I assure you, this nectar is far better than any our Lord ever encountered —Geoffrey Turner's private stock."

"Behind me, Satan! God has told me not to imbibe spirits. I obey His commands."

"You personally receive instructions from God Almighty, do you?" Sparrow asked, leaning solicitously toward MacPherson.

"Yes."

"Ah. Well. I *am* happy to note that the rest of you are not opposed. You see, it's a day of celebration hereabouts, and it *would* be a shame prematurely to end it—even over the misfortune lately visited upon our doorstep. I trust, Mr. Jerkin, that you will not hold the loss of your friend against us. We of HOPE are truly grateful for the remuneration you have provided for the—um, misplaced silver. We would like you to know that we wish you to enjoy yourself the few hours we will allow you to remain upon these premises."

"Thompson?" Jerkin gulped his champagne. "No great loss, Thompson."

"Alas, I wish I could say the same about dear Frederick. I shall have to train Otto not to be so militant about his duties." Raising his thin eyebrows, Sparrow said, "You understand that we of HOPE, so few in number, *do* need protection? The very sort of creatures we employ now, for years we were intent on destroying! Well, as dear Geoffrey used to say, 'Permutations, dear Sparrow, are unlimited in a mutating existence.'"

Sparrow seemed to be lighted from within by a wonderfully controlled inner fire; fueled, it seemed, by alcohol. Geoffrey Turner had definitely been his schoolmaster.

"Where are the others?" Penton asked. "How many are you?"

"What *are* you celebrating?" Jennifer chimed in, a little flushed with the champagne.

"The others number approximately sixty, not counting the odd wife or child. We are not all bachelors, you see. I will introduce you all at dinner tonight. Part of the celebration of Geoffrey Turner's birthday!"

Oliver brightened. "You mean today would have been Turner's birthday." Oliver darkened. "But . . . but he wasn't really born, was he?"

"Excuse me?"

"Never mind." Of course. The people of HOPE didn't realize that Geoffrey Turner had been a mandroid.

"No, Geoffrey Turner never knew exactly when his birthday was. Whenever he felt like having a party, he claimed it was his birthday. Convenient, no?"

"Yes."

"And you all, save for Mr. Jerkin, are of course invited." He turned to the thief. "I *am* sorry, but we fear for our silverware."

"That's all right. Just give me some food and some drink and I'll be pushing off."

"How congenial of you. I believe all that can be arranged." He smiled slyly. "We can even escort you past the basilisk." He stepped beside MacPherson. "I trust, sir, that you will stay as long as your arm takes to heal. We wish to make whatever amends necessary."

"I confess," MacPherson said wearily, settling into an overstuffed chair. "I feel a touch weak."

"Splendid. You may all stay as long as you wish." He twirled toward Oliver. "It will give you, Mr. Dolan, the opportunity to see what we're about. I'd be happy to be your guide, for this place is a treasure trove of Styx. The Holy Order to Preserve the Empire has been extant for some time, you know. Five centuries of opposition to the rule of Hedley Nicholas over Styx. Five hundred years of dedicated monster-killing. Fifty decades of the righteous march to shed light upon the benighted peoples of this poor planet." He finished his champagne and winked as he raised the glass. "But in *my* decade, I must admit I've enjoyed this most."

"You've been out then, destroying the beasties of Satan?"

97

MacPherson asked, his voice noticeably weakened by his present state.

"Me?" Sparrow swept back his locks and assumed a horrified pose.

"But I thought you chaps rallied in vans, searching for the minions of Hell with electronic weapons devised by Geoffrey Turner." Penton was beginning to feel uneasy.

"Good Lord, no!" The man was scandalized. "Turner was the only crazy one among us! None of *us* ventured out after our initial experiences with Turner!"

Oliver blinked. "Experiences? Yes, come to think of it, how *did* you get here?"

"Well, naturally, some of us were *born* here, but quite often that sort leave as soon as they are able for—um, more *conventional* communities. Actually, more than half of us here now arrived because of Turner. Sorceror's apprentices, don't you know, Lord Dolan." He tapped Oliver's arm softly with each word. "Just like you!"

"I don't take your meaning," Oliver returned.

"Your whole story! Absolutely typical Turner trick! Only in your case, it should be said, *somehow* it succeeded. And now! Now, poor Geoffrey is gone. He didn't *preserve* what was left of the Empire. In killing Satan, he's irrevocably destroyed whatever was left of it—most noticeably his own attitudes." He spoke to Oliver in a confidential manner. "You see, dear boy, Turner rather fancied young lads."

Oliver blanched. "That's—that's just not true!"

"No! No, no, no! Not *that* way. He just enjoyed a malleable mind. He reveled in being the father image, don't you know, of an impressionable youngster. Even a few girls . . . when he could *get* them. However, in his journeys, he usually managed to come across an adolescent or two who actually was impressed with his glorious tales. He encouraged them to tag along. At the end of the foray—if they hadn't been killed—he'd bring them here. Naturally, they could not very well return to the "normal" Victorian way of life—not when wonderland was promised. Remember your own enthusiasm upon arriving here, Mr. Dolan. I was quite the same way."

"You traveled with Turner?" Penton asked. "You hardly seem the type."

Sparrow raised his eyebrows, then pouted a bit. "In my time I was *quite* good. One had to be to survive with Turner for any length of time."

"Hold a moment. From what you've said, it seems that you knew about Turner? . . ."

"What? That he was a mandroid? But of course! On his layovers here, special attendants saw to his maintenance. This, you see, Oliver, was Geoffrey Turner's home, his family. He could return to us and be among friends. He was patriarch to us all! The news of his corporeal passing, though, sad as it is, was inevitable. That the bastard lived *this* long is astonishing; that he accomplished his goal was a miracle. That ship from space he ranted about—we thought it a product of a warped mind. Well, you never know. You never know."

"But what about *now!* It hasn't ended, Mr. Sparrow. Awful things are happening on Styx and HOPE offers the only hope of preventing a dark age."

"Would anyone care for some more bubbly?" Sparrow asked congenially.

Empty glasses were eagerly pushed forward.

Sparrow, ever the proper host, filled.

"Aren't you listening to me, Sparrow," Oliver asked indignantly. "You're living on Geoffrey Turner's legacy. This world needs you now more than ever! A disease is changing humans into vampires! The author of this plague seems to be seeking control of Styx; Anziel Dubrelizy may return at any moment with who knows what; armies of men and nightcreatures stand ready to march; and you are going to sit on your rear ends and slurp champagne?"

"What good would it do to try otherwise? We live a good life here, Mr. Dolan. We try to enjoy it. We are not bad people, nor do we intend to be selfish. Qualified visitors—like your excellent company here—are welcome to the wealth of knowledge accumulated by our forebears and, of course, Mr. Turner. Our only duty is to guard this wealth of knowledge. We have *our* purpose, Lord Dolan. Are you so sure of *yours?*"

"And what's to prevent HOPE'S being overrun? You have to do *something!*"

"We have endured some centuries. If we come to an end, so be it. However, I believe we have sufficient means to protect our interests. If you care to take from our store of knowledge whatever means you think sufficient to curtail the spread of this disease—"

"You mean that you might have *methods?*"

Sparrow shrugged helplessly. "That is very hard to say. We shall have to consult our expert on that."

"Who is . . . ?"

"You will meet the expert at the festivities this evening," Sparrow announced coyly. He extracted a watch from his vest pocket. "Only an hour away! Now, if you will accompany me, I will show you to the guest quarters." He cast an amused eye toward Jerkin. "And you, sir, I will show the door!"

"A TOAST!"

"To our guests, who have brought us the story of our beloved Geoffrey Turner's final hours, and the full story of his victory over our nemesis, Hedley Nicholas!"

The men seated around the several banquet tables booed the name, aided robustly by the women. The crowd then cheered exuberantly for their guests.

Only Penton acknowledged the accolade. The manservant stood, bowed formally, and then seated himself. Oliver felt a trifle uneasy.

The people of HOPE were certainly not what he'd expected. If he'd thought Sparrow strange, he now realized that the man's affected manner was positively normal compared to that of his fellows.

Seated about Oliver were perhaps fifty or sixty men and women of various ages. All wore attire of outrageous and colorful variety, rendering the affair more a costume party than a formal dinner.

Sparrow raised his hands for silence, in the process revealing a yellow silk vest beneath his swallow-tailed coat. The mingled voices of the assembly became mere murmurs. Satisfied, he began his address. "We are privileged to have the company of our guests for a short period, that Mr. MacPherson's arm might heal. During this time, a stenographer will record Lord Dolan's testimony that we might have in our archives the final chapter of our illustrious founder's adventures. In the meantime, I have assured them all—Miss Jennifer Eden, Mr. Roald MacPherson, Mr. Caspar Penton"—he pointed to each as he spoke—"that while Mr. Dolan dictates, they may have the run of our castle. I am sure we will all be pleased to show them about, sharing in our work and in our play."

Polite applause sufficed as agreement. A top hat took leave of a bobbing head, tumbling into a nearly empty tureen of soup. It was retrieved by the owner to the guffaws and chuckles of his companions. Mr. Sparrow cleared his throat theatrically, then held his lapels in a suitable speech-making manner. Through half-frame glasses, he peered down his nose to the agenda. "Now, as our sumptuous repast is, indeed, past, and our last-minute welcomes accorded, we will resume our traditional agenda."

"Here, here!" a man in a powdered wig cried from the back.

"Yes. As is our custom on Turner Day, representatives of the various cells will present their reports on the year's activities. These reports and their documentation will be stored against the ravages of age in the preserving chamber. Now. We will begin with a general address by the Honorable Mr. Beadle, the elected mayor of this august community. Mr. Beadle, would you step forward?"

Oliver turned to Penton. "*These* are Geoffrey Turner's trainees?"

"Disillusioned?"

"Astonished."

"Watch, Oliver. And think about what I told you before."

With much rattling of furniture and dishes, a big-bellied man with elaborately coiffed hair raised himself from his seat and waddled to the dais, hand clasped about a goblet. He slurped a final gulp of wine. "As you know," he said, "things have changed a bit here on Styx. But let me say here and now that HOPE has not changed. Nor will it ever, as long as our good citizens continue in their freely chosen paths shown to us by Geoffrey Turner." His dewlaps quivered with righteous pride. "The chosen few remain few. Remain chosen. So it will continue as long as stout hearts and nimble minds prevail among our number!"

He paused and nodded, self-satisfied, at the applause.

"As we have heard from our guests, Hedley Nicholas is finally dead. His nightcreatures released. Result? Chaos. But what do we have to say about chaos, my friends and colleagues!"

A white-haired old man stood. He waved his cane. His greatcoat wavered about his emaciated form. "It cannot be tolerated!"

"Nor will it be!" Mayor Beadle bellowed. " 'Nor will the tides of nothingness which lap at our very souls and shoe soles be accommodated.' That, dear people, is from the very mouth of Geoffrey Turner. It is our sworn duty, our *privilege* to continue our lives embracing . . ."

And so it went. Oliver quickly ceased to listen. In a like manner passed the report of the Gaming Society. However, the next speaker was the august chairman of the Science Society. Oliver's interest was immediately aroused. White hair bloomed above the fellow's receding brow. He wore a rumpled worsted suit and industriously chalked complex equations upon a squeaking blackboard. Pages of his speech dropped from time to time from his hands as he hopped about amid the dust of his work. The audience seemed to respect him immensely, and even those who fell asleep were polite enough not to snore. As far as Oliver could tell, the talk involved aspects of physics and astronomy and the essential underpinnings of mathematics. The man's thesis, it seemed, was the universe had always existed and always would in a constant flux and wane of interchanging energy and matter.

By this time Oliver had consumed a goodly amount of wine. When Dr. Plaster asked for questions, Oliver had the temerity to ask how his thesis related to the situation on Styx. In particular he inquired if the doctor knew anything of biochemistry and the plague of vampirism now sweeping the planet.

His question was greeted with a severe glare from the doctor, and disapproving gazes from the assembled. "Science, sir, is a study unto itself, pure as pure can be. One who sullies himself by addressing inconsequential *problems* will sink into the quagmire of irrationalism that is the human condition. Have you not been listening? Can you not deduce the meaning of what I have to say? We are merely momentary vibrant specks of dust in the cosmic eye. We matter not at all in the scheme of things!"

He bowed to the applause of his fellow society members.

Oliver would have risen to challenge the doctor, but he was restrained by Penton, who whispered, "Never argue with a dust speck. Quite unrewarding."

To his left, Jennifer slept prettily; but she roused for the next speaker, the town's sociologist. Unfortunately, sociology at HOPE consisted of systematized gossip about the Order's principals, so Jennifer was soon fetchingly at peace once more.

Sociology eventually yielded to poetry, whose chairperson read some wretched verse. Fiction related the titles of the several short stories and novels written by the populace over the past year, noting with pride how quality had not been affected at all by the "Changes Outside." Awards were distributed for the best of the year—in twenty categories— to general applause. The losers both threw food at the judges.

Art was displayed, with suitable reportage. High-minded

adjective flew from rapidly gibbering mouths. Fashion paraded. . . .

Oliver found it an endlessly complicated, endlessly stupid society. The ceremonies were interminable, the drinking endless. When the final speaker made his way to the podium, half the citizens lay upon the floor.

The last speaker—a Mr. Thaddeus Hunter—spoke briefly of the Order's goals, particularly in agriculture and trading, saving his surprise for last. "Before the party gets underway, we have a special treat for you. The Keeper of the Mechanisms has finally repaired the Einstein, including its speech synthesizer. So we have a very special visitor from the past this evening—a person I'm sure we—" he hiccoughed. " 'Scuse me. We all remember fondly."

Hunter waved his hand to two men who stood in the rear of the room. They promptly wheeled out a table on which was a large box covered by a white sheet. An extension cord was plugged into a wall outlet.

His interest aroused, Oliver elbowed the drowsing Penton, noting faintly the feverish intensity of the quite-awake MacPherson.

"What's a—whatever he called it?"

"An Einstein? Goodness knows. I don't."

A box.

Knobs and switches and levers and assorted bumps covered it, save for a round screen upon which a sine wave wiggled. Lights blinked randomly across the box's surface. One antenna sprouted from each side, the final touches of oddness to this strange contraption.

Mr. Thaddeus Hunter pulled up his sleeves.

He touched a button.

Something like ears emerged from the square head and an orchestra struck up "God Save the Queen." Those asleep were quickly awakened and stood solemnly.

The anthem finished with a flourish, and the sine wave upon the oscilloscope divided into three and wavered wildly. The lights blinked more rapidly, seemingly in a complex pattern.

Hunter tapped more buttons. "You in there or not, old chap?"

The sine waves disappeared. A single word took their place:

YES

"All your circuits in place? The engineers treat you right?"

EVERYTHING IS FINE

"Well then, dear boy, why don't you *say* something?"

VOCAL CIRCUITS MANUAL

These words flashed twice, then were replaced.

PUSH THE BUTTON, YOU ASS

"Oh, right. Sorry." Hunter found the correct control, pushed it.

"Thank you," a well-synthesized voice said. The intonation was flat, yet there was something oddly familiar to Oliver about the speech rhythm.

"Our apologies for the time it took to fix you," Hunter continued. "But since so much comes from you in the way of instructions for maintenance, when you yourself went on the blink we had to consult operational booklets."

"Quite so. Einsteins *are* a bit beyond you. If only the Impressor were here."

"We have visitors with news of him."

"Indeed. Who? And what is the news?"

"We will introduce their data soon. I don't know how you're going to take it."

"Take it? I was not programmed for actual emotions."

"True, but—"

"But what?"

"Dammit, sometimes you seem just like him!" Hunter said, shaking his head. "I mean, you don't know how hard it's been with you gone. And your voice isn't right." He adjusted knobs. "There."

The machine spoke again. "I say, would you mind turning on my eyes so I can bloody well see what's going on?"

Oliver stood, knocking over two empty wine bottles. That voice—he knew now where he recognized it from. He grabbed Penton by the collar and shook him. "Penton! My God, Penton!"

Penton blinked, quite perplexed. "What's wrong?"

"That voice!" Oliver said. "That's Geoffrey Turner's voice!"

Breathing shallowly, Vlad, Lord Paler walked among the mechanisms of control, his telepathy machines. He was slightly stooped, grimacing as if experiencing pain. A few lines had etched themselves into his previously young, smooth face.

He held his hands behind his back as he inspected. He paced slowly among the vampire lab technicians who monitored the readings upon the banks of machinery, holding clipboards and making notes.

Dr. Mendelsohn had only just released him from confinement. His attack had been sudden and inexplicable. Wrenching pain had suffused him. Knives seemed to have slashed at every fiber of his being. He had, for a moment, felt *possessed*. Something seemed to have taken hold for a fleeting moment, and he had lost that quality he most cherished: control.

Dr. Mendelsohn, however, had diagnosed no internal trouble.

"It has something to do with the component the homunculus stole," Paler had immediately decided. "Its absence is leaving me vulnerable to *something*." At Mendelsohn's suggestion broad-spectrum rf analyses were made, but nothing seemed to have a positive correlation.

"A freak occurrence," Mendelsohn had decided.

There was no recurrence and Paler recovered his health. His other operations continued to run smoothly. His representatives and spies among the developing nation-states were performing admirably. One developing nation, a place called Amnia, even appeared willing to form an alliance— his advice and knowledge in return for a measure of power and a slice of the spoils when war finally came and Amnia successfully conquered. How fascinating it all was, this jockeying for power among human societies. However, war would be *much* more interesting, with all its violence and intrigue.

New vampires joined his ranks daily and were controlled by his delightful machines. How good they made him feel even now as he walked among them. Without them, the dead would simply stay dead, shambling hosts of virus colonies with no animating will. The machines tracked every individual, controlling all according to General Orders and Standard Operating Procedures supplied by Paler from his computer control station.

Oh, if Satan could only see him now!

Nicholas had called him "son." He recalled that now. Son. From time to time the man ensnared within the computer system would moan, becoming almost lucid. "My God, my God, what is happening to me?" he would say. Or, "My name is Nicholas. Hedley Nicholas!" Paler had observed several such tortured moments, had stood by the vat-like arrangement and held the man's withered hand,

The old man would sometimes regain consciousness and, sensing Paler's presence, a ghost of a smile would cross his twisted features. "My son. I can talk to you, my son. This world will be ours together. I have created you as my equal that we might share it. My dream is your dream, no? To create the Universe anew, according to my grand vision. But sometimes, son, even a fallen angel has dreams. Terrible dreams he cannot explain. If the Enemy vanquishes me, you must carry on in my place. This is why I have taught you so much."

"Yes, Father," Paler would say, patting the old hand comfortingly.

The old fool! The wretched half-man! Hadn't he realized that to make a creature in his own image with full knowledge and no delusions would insure rebellion? At first, Paler had attempted to introduce his innovations slowly, to make them sound as if Nicholas had thought of them. The old one, however, would have none of it. Paler acquiesced always, but resentment grew in his heart. He humored Satan as best he could, but secretly continued his own plan. The best thing for Nicholas, he'd decided, was to have him put out to peaceful pasture. Once Paler was in complete control, he reasoned, he might actually work on his creator, ease some of the man's agony. Perhaps a few operations would set him right mentally, make him rational and alert once more.

Then Paler could have a true father.

Then his terrible loneliness might be assuaged.

But Paler had been betrayed, his rebellion nipped in the bud. He'd been brought before Satan in chains. The old man had wept openly. "Because you are my son, I will not destroy you. Perhaps a cold imprisonment of many years will destroy your ungratefulness, your lack of appreciation, to your betterment!"

"But Your Glory! Is it not natural for the son of the Great Rebeller to rebel himself?"

"Have you not learned? We despise nature. Take him to the chamber I have prepared."

And so Paler had been removed to cold sleep and there imprisoned with his pain and his hatred for his creator.

How angry Paler had been to hear of the old creature's demise. Revenge had been denied him. Yet he had felt grief, for no one in this world could understand him as his father had. . . .

"Are you well, Lord Paler?" A servant hovered above him, expressionless. A lot the bastard really cared.

"Yes. Yes, I'm fine." He stood, smoothing his trousers. "How are my machines?"

"All fully functional, Lord. We are up to half capacity at the moment. All is performing just as you designed it. We wait now only for your tactical directions. Otherwise the creatures will simply attack and sup at random."

Half capacity! Already! That meant, in the Phase One infection area, five thousand souls were already under his command. "Hmm. We shall have to begin work on additional equipment earlier than scheduled. That is, unless our losses impede growth."

"They are only two percent higher than your initial estimate, Lord." The vampire technician held his head proudly.

"Twenty-two percent! Very fine! As soon as the dens grow to community takeovers, the percentage loss will lower drastically."

"Until the wars, sir."

"Ah, but that has been taken into account. By that time the infection will have spread so far—through Phase Ten by my judgment—that despite measures taken by those who realize what is happening, the progression of slaves will be unstoppable. Except, of course, by ourselves."

"Ourselves, Your Lordship?" The vampire blinked in consternation.

"Certainly. We don't want everyone on this world to be a vampire. How boring! Besides, what would our dear slaves drink then? No, if you think this"—he motioned toward his machines—"is all I have planned for the world, you are quite wrong."

"Yes, Your Greatness."

"Oh, do come off that stuff, my friend." Paler patted his servant's shoulder. "I know you know your place. Now then. Strategy— Oh, by the way, have you been keeping a bead on the jabberwock I sent out after the Dolan chap?"

"Yes, sir. After that incident at sea—"

"Yes. Good thing poor Darkwing knew how to swim."

"Yes. Well, he *has* picked up the trail of its quarry. Found a few trolls they'd killed."

Paler rubbed his hands together. "Excellent! *Super!* So we should prepare for a confrontation. However, we had best set to work on locating another jabberwock, just in case. Beam that message over the network immediately. Should one of our vampires encounter a jabberwock—"

Paler smiled to himself. "Tell him we've employment waiting at top wages."

Somewhere, relays clicked, a tuner was spun at random.
Radio waves were propagated, seeking like vengeful ghosts.

ACT THREE

"Where the bee sucks, there suck I."

—William Shakespeare
The Tempest

III: 1

MR. SPARROW turned to Oliver Dolan. "Of course it's Geoffrey Turner's voice. That's his Einstein." He pointed to the computer box.

"Einstein?" Penton sounded bemused.

"Yes. Clever little phrase. It's an Electronic Mind Clone. Get it? E=MC squared. Or in this case, doubled. Einstein's theory of relativity. Quite simply it's an imprint of Turner's personality and knowledge made quite some time back, just in case he failed to return to his flock."

"You mean—" Oliver said, staring at the blinking lights of the thing. "You mean that this box is Turner's mental twin?"

"Oh, it's not intelligent. It just *seems* that way. No soul at all!"

"I resent that!" the box said.

Sparrow shrugged. "We humor it."

"I should like you, sir, to define intelligence!"

Sparrow spoke from the side of his mouth, confidentially. "We've been through all this before, box." He minced up to the box and leaned against it casually. "Sorry, old chap. You are, of course, intelligent."

"Quite right," the box replied.

"And you are who?" Sparrow examined his manicured fingernails.

"Why, Geoffrey Turner, of course!" The voice sent chills through Oliver. "Originally the historical mandroid Herbert George Wells. Would you care for the other names I have gone by?"

"That won't be necessary. How long have you been inside that box?" Sparrow inquired. "I ask for the benefit of our guests."

"I have been programmed into these circuits over the past four hundred years. My original found my body in the same place he located much of the equipment he utilized later in his efforts against Hedley Nicholas. After his founding of this Holy Order, he placed me here. Upon each return from his travels, he transcribed into my memory banks the exact details through direct mind transfer utilizing the read/scan cap in my Compartment A." The voice

113

paused a moment, as if considering. "Actually, I believe, as usual, we are dealing here with different levels of semantics. I am a direct reflection of Geoffrey Turner's mind, including his memory, his thought patterns, the various levels of his being up to his last recording over two years ago. I admit, I am only a duplicate of all the aspects of the mandroid who called himself Geoffrey Turner. Turner thought himself an intelligent creature; therefore, I do. Whether I truly am or not is moot."

"Herbert." Sparrow turned about, addressing the visitors. "That's what we call it, to prevent confusion. Herbert, I should like to present some guests of ours who bring news of your—ah—programmer. Are your ocular units functioning properly?"

"Yes. I can see quite well now."

Sparrow introduced each, Oliver last. When it came his turn, Oliver was strangely hurt that the machine did not recognize him. But of course his disappointment was foolish. The last time Turner had programmed the thing, he had not yet met Oliver Dolan. Still, it *was* a troubling experience.

Sparrow said, "They have brought news."

"I deduce that my creator has finally succumbed. Since Satan is no longer in control of the nightcreatures—an event that we did not foresee, alas—I presume that Geoffrey Turner Prime was also successful in destroying our nemesis, Hedley Nicholas."

"You are not disturbed by this?"

"It is what my creator wished. Naturally, it is odd to have no further input, but then my function was to serve as his surrogate once this event occurred."

"Geoffrey Turner is dead. Long live Geoffrey Turner, eh?" Sparrow commented wryly.

"I am the storage place of his persona and his memory. In me reside his recollections of the Second Victorian Empire. My purpose is to recall those histories as example to the civilization that may grow on this planet."

"It's going to be a little shocked to hear about Anziel's civilization," Penton commented quietly to Oliver.

"Pardon me?" the Einstein said.

"Oh, nothing. We'll have a long talk with you tomorrow," Oliver said. "Would that be all right, Mr. Sparrow? It's been quite a day, and I think we're all a little tired. I've certainly had a bit too much to drink to hold the kind of conversation I think appropriate."

"Very well. I trust that you find your quarters suitable," Sparrow said.

"Quite," Penton replied.

Jennifer, half asleep, leaned against Oliver. As Sparrow turned off the machine and covered it again with the sheet, Oliver helped her to her room.

She was too tired to change. Oliver tucked her into bed.

"Oh, Ollie, it's so nice sleeping in a bed again. It's . . . it's almost like everything is going to be wonderful."

"It will, Jenny," Oliver said, stroking her hair. "I promise it will."

"Oliver, I . . . I feel so . . . so very strange . . . taking what I need from you." She touched his bandaged hand gently.

"If I needed it, you'd give it to me too, wouldn't you?"

"Of course!" She smiled softly up at him. "Would you like to stay here tonight? It's a very nice bed." She chuckled softly. "It's not as if we haven't shared a bed before." She paused. "Oliver?"

"Yes."

"You're infected with the disease as well. Yet you only *give*. Why don't you want to take?"

"I suppose it's not that far advanced yet, Jenny. Pray MacPherson gets us to the cure before it does."

"I'm here if you need it, Oliver," Jennifer said. "My blood is your blood now. It's like we're parts of the same person."

"I don't know, Jenny. It's not right." He shook his head, troubled. "Just not right."

"You give so much, yet take so little."

Oliver swallowed. His mouth was dry. "You get to sleep now. Just resist such thoughts. Go to sleep."

"All right, Ollie." She turned over on her side as he switched off the light. "G'night."

"Good night, Jenny." He went to the door, then stopped. Moonbeams filled the window, steaming through and settling on her head, which poked from the covers sweetly, innocently, contentedly.

He gazed at her a moment, bit his lip hard, until he felt the taste of blood. He had to force himself to turn away and retreat to his chambers.

Oliver dreamed.
His dreams were all red.

. . . believe in the Lord thy God or suffer the pit of damnation after death . . .

The dreams bellowed with obnoxious hymns.

. . . thou must not . . .

The faces of the ministers who had formed his religious and moral thought glared down at him. They fused together into the quiet demanding face of his mother, the retreating, haunted face of his father.

. . . for the Lord thy God is a jealous God . . .

"Oliver! Oliver Dolan!"

He started. He would have cried out if not for the hand that clamped his mouth, stifling his voice.

He choked and tried to struggle.

"Do not be alarmed, Oliver Dolan. I mean no harm."

Calmed only a bit, Oliver released his stiffness. The hand departed. A light flickered up. The smell of melting wax. A burning wick. A small candle, being lit.

The glow spilled up to flow over the harsh angles of Roald MacPherson's face. He wore no hat. His hair was mussed. An uncharacteristic look of desperation masked his face. His left arm hung free of its sling, but it was still bandaged.

Oliver sat up in bed, the covers flopping down around his lap softly. His warmth gave way rapidly before the cold of the room.

"What are you doing here?"

"I must speak to you." A shuddering hand sifted through tangled hair. "I am having . . . difficulty."

"What's wrong?" Oliver had never seen the man in such a state. He looked frantic, where before he had seemed to be calm and certain of himself and his purpose.

"I bear another message from God."

"Nothing unusual in that. You get them all the time."

"Yes. Yes, but not like this one. He . . . He did not sound the same."

"Are you sure this message was from . . . um, *God*, MacPherson."

"Yes. The voice was the same. But it . . . it babbled, Oliver Dolan. It made no sense. I could only understand part of what it said. This does not follow what I had assumed before. This machine—this machine that talks is troublesome."

"Listen, MacPherson." Oliver put a comforting hand to the troubled man's shoulder. "I wasn't so sure of it before, but you're a human like the rest of us."

116

"I was created by the Lord God for His purposes!" the man said, attempting indignation but failing. "I—I—"

"I understand. You're confused by what you think on your own, by what you fear. It's not a black-and-white world, believe me. This voice you hear. God's voice. How do you think it comes to you."

"Why, spiritually, of course."

"Isn't it also possible that it could be an implanted radio! You've seen radios, MacPherson. Here—maybe other places. Perhaps you've a transceiver in your head."

"Blasphemy! Tools of the Devil!" But his voice broke. He put his head in his hand and began to weep. "I cannot *believe* this. It goes against all I am!"

"Not tools of the Devil, man. Just *tools!*"

"My faith is being tested," MacPherson muttered, quite wretchedly.

Oliver gave MacPherson a moment to compose himself. "What were you saying before? God, babbling? Babbling about what?"

"Machines. He used many strange terms—I did not understand. However, when I asked Him to make Himself clear to His poor servant, there was a long pause, then a simple order."

"What was the order?"

"*That* was what was so puzzling. He asked me to sin. He said, 'My servant, I want you to steal the Einstein. They will never let you have it if you ask. Steal it, my servant. *Steal* it!'"

III: 2

>=0=0==0==0=0==0=0==0==0==0==0=

THE WOMAN handled it expertly, using confident, sure strokes.

The pencil made steady scratching sounds at the paper as she wrote. Oliver admired her professional attitude as she transcribed his account of the last weeks of Geoffrey Turner's life. Very pleasant to gaze upon as well was the brunette Lydia Burthington. She had been born in the Order a quarter of a century before, she explained over the late-morning tea that prefaced the session. At nineteen she'd departed to marry a man in a neighboring community, but he'd succumbed to a nightcreature. Lydia returned to HOPE and undertook the duties of recorder, a capacity in which she'd served with distinction.

She had a matter-of-fact handsomeness, a sturdy beauty made mature by a hint of crow's feet around her eyes and wrinkles about her small mouth. Her nose was just a nose, no lilt to it, perhaps a bit too broad at the bridge. Her cheeks were pale, unpronounced. Yet somehow all this ordinariness of feature conspired to present a face quite pretty, its effects strongly communicated by the chemistry of her personality. Lydia Burthington plainly was aware of herself not merely as a woman, but as a person. She either liked people or did not, dealing with them honestly and forthrightly. That she *liked* Oliver was clear; that Oliver found her fascinating he could not deny. He enjoyed the two days they'd spent together working on his account. In fact, he was sorry that he was almost finished. His suggestion that, for better detail, he should be rigorously questioned about his story for one final session the next day was not so much for posterity as to spend more time with her.

Lydia seemed gently amused by this ploy, and agreed to the questioning.

Oliver, his dramatic sense increased with his desire to impress the woman, gave an emotional description of Geoffrey Turner's death, then lapsed into moody silence, gripping the wooden arms of the chair in which he slouched.

Lydia finished the last of the shorthand, accompanied only by the sounds of the old grandfather clock in the corner. She then neatly stacked her work. Oliver sensed her stare. He met her gaze. She had bright, welcoming hazel eyes. "An astonishing story," she said softly. "It must require much of a person to experience things like this."

"I was frightened for a while, Lydia. Then I just went numb. The violence didn't matter—you learn to accept things, I think, if you have to."

"The remarkable adaptability of the human creature!" She picked up the manuscript. "Well, perhaps I should begin typing."

"No. Please. We're going to leave in a few days. MacPherson's wound is healing rapidly. I'd like to hear more about you." He stood and tapped the pile of papers. "You can type this up anytime, can't you?"

"Of course." She cast her eyes toward the tea tray. "The tea is cold, but there's enough for two more cups."

Oliver got his cup and saucer. With a dry swoosh of dark skirts, Lydia retrieved the tea.

"I hope your journey meets with success," she said as she poured.

"If not, you certainly won't hear from *us* about it."

"Yes. It *is* serious, isn't it? Jennifer— There is something wrong with her. I can tell."

Oliver crossed to the window and stared pensively into the empty courtyard. He held his bandaged hand against the sun, which hung just above the ivy-covered castle walls. A little blood had seeped through the fresh gauze. "She's a dear person. I can't—I can't imagine her gone."

"The disease you spoke of—genetic vampirism. That's why Dr. Adamson has been running tests on her, isn't it?" She sounded concerned.

"I've got it as well, though not so seriously. My system seems to be fighting it better than hers. We're following MacPherson to where he claims we can be cured."

"I see. She's very young, Oliver, chimeric. I was like that once. Don't take what she *does* so seriously. Try and understand who she *is*. We all need security, Oliver. Sometimes we cling too hard for it, and in our desperation we kill our chances for the love we crave." She looked at him appraisingly. "You're quite an attractive young man, Oliver. Jennifer need not be the one for you."

Oliver looked away. "I—I have an obligation to Jennifer. I love her dearly. I promised myself that no harm would come to her."

"I suppose I find you attractive myself, Oliver." She
119

smiled calmly. "Another predatory female sniffing about you, dear boy!"

"What can I say?" Oliver mumbled, flustered. "I'm flattered. I like you as well."

"Excellent. Let's leave it at that. You have Jennifer—or rather, she has you. When that stops, we shall continue in this vein. For now, we are acquaintances verging on friendship."

"You were going to tell me about yourself."

"Yes. As a matter of fact, I can rather sympathize with Jennifer because—"

She was interrupted by the door opening.

Penton, Dr. Adamson, and Jennifer entered.

Jennifer was rolling down one of her sleeves. Wearing an odd expression, she gave Oliver just a glance, then drifted to the tea tray in search of sweets. She selected a chocolate chip cookie, then sat in one of the chairs. Her manner was distant.

Penton said, "Well, the doctor here has had a look at that blood sample of yours, Oliver. And at Jennifer's."

"Well?" Oliver asked.

Producing a hand-rolled cigarette from the pocket of his jacket, the doctor said, "It seems simple enough in principle. As you may know, little beasties run about our bloodstreams. Red cells, which carry the oxygen through liquid plasma to keep a body's tissues going; white cells, rather like police, attack diseases and abnormal red cells, generally keeping things shipshape. Well, now. What *this* disease evidently does is to introduce a third kind of cell. God knows what they actually are, but for some reason the white cells can't distinguish them all the time from the red cells, though when they *do*, they off the little buggers good and proper. These new cells—let's call them vampire cells, just to keep our terms simple—are fascinating. They're parasites, doing not a damned thing for the body and chewing up food and oxygen at that. Evidently what is happening in Miss Eden is that the vampire cells have begun to feast randomly on her red blood cells. Result? Rather like anemia. Their goal, though, is not death."

"No?"

"No. Actually, in the initial phases of the disease, they seem innocent enough. *If* left on their own." The doctor puffed contemplatively on his cigarette. "Are you aware that cells form . . . colonies? We've very important bacteria

120

in our digestive system, for example, that help us process the substances of our food."

"Alas," Penton said, "the education in science is understandably poor in most communities."

"Of course. I learned what I know from Mr. Turner. Much of what we've produced here in the way of findings is the work of his Einstein. What a useful piece of work, that!

"At any rate, as these vampire cells grow in number, they form a kind of colony, a separate network, linked throughout the body particularly in the brain. Once this colony is fully developed, it simply exists. The hypothesis of the Einstein, one in which I concur, is that these cells, when fully developed, are mirrored in the activity of the host. Which means that an emotional and physical dependence develops—rather like a drug habit—for blood. Now this *can* be animal blood. But our guess is that *human* blood is much more satisfying. Fortunately for you both, the colony is not yet formed in either of you. I *am* puzzled at Jennifer's state. The vampire cells are curiously static in her, as if somehow . . . what's the proper term? Yes. *Satiated*. However, we know so little."

"A colony?" Penton said. "Does that not imply some sort of communication network—cooperation?"

"Precisely. Our bodies are essentially conglomerations of cooperating colonies that work according to programs supervised by the neurochemical overseer, the brain. I'm glad you asked about it, because our sensors *have* indicated that some strange electromagnetic activity occurs among the vampire cells. They seem to communicate as two radios communicate—rather like telepathy." He looked at Jennifer, then turned his gaze to Oliver. "Have you two ever felt as if you knew what the other was thinking?"

Blushing a bit, Jennifer said, "I—I believe so."

The doctor smiled understandingly. "And you thought it merely love's little messages. No, you're quite right. This would have to be close-range transfer. *Very* close."

Oliver blushed. No one noticed.

"All right, let's take the *given:* some—some Vampire Lord, as you call him. Obviously, he's aware of the processes involved, including what occurs if the person hosting the parasitic cells dies. The colony essentially takes over! A pseudomind develops, utilizing what's left of the person's personality, and maintains the body's functions, but on a different level. What do you have? A genuine vampire, with the ability to pass on more cells to another human. Thus spreading the disease. This—"

"Wait a moment, though," Penton interrupted. "Why do the vampires crave blood, then? Does it have any function?"

"My guess is that vampirism transforms some parts of the body. I haven't one on hand to dissect, but I wouldn't be at all surprised if the esophagus led to a new organ which processes the blood and channels it into the rebuilt circulatory system. The vampire probably becomes a new kind of human being, albeit a zombie motivated only by blood lust, patterned only in necessary particulars after the man or woman whose body it uses. And since a vampire really reproduces itself by spreading bits of the colony even as it feeds upon another's blood, I would not be at all surprised if it possessed sensory apparatus to gain a kind of pleasure from the act of taking blood. All this is speculation, of course. But it *sounds* right."

"You were saying about the Vampire Lord?" Oliver asked.

"Right. It seems possible that this fellow actually designed the cells, programmed them for just this sort of thing. The question is, *why?* Each vampire could, of course, survive on its own. Obviously they prefer to cluster for protection—perhaps even for companionship. These groups should manifest increased telepathic power. I suppose that if there were enough of them, left on their own, some kind of mass mind might develop, an intelligence. Certainly an individual vampire is not intelligent—merely a biological robot. Now. Obviously there is a reason for this in the mind of the creator—this Vampire Lord—and it seems obvious to me that he has the power to communicate with these new beings, *control* them. No doubt through some sort of computer arrangement with transmitters and receivers enough to contact individual vampires."

Oliver said, "I don't understand a lot of what you've said, but I can say that these creatures *are* controlled. That it's by this Vampire Lord seems obvious enough. The question remains—is there any way that can be developed to kill off these vampire cells as you call them? Some medicine?"

"The Einstein sees that as a possibility, but much time and experimentation are necessary before any answer is certain." He smiled. "I've spoken to Mr. Sparrow, and to the others of our board. We'd be glad to provide room and board while we attack the problem."

Oliver said, "Why, that's very gracious of you, Doctor!

I can't think of a more comfortable way to end our journey. We'd be happy to accept your invitation."

Penton positively beamed. Jennifer was busy staring at a group of animal figurines on a nearby dresser. She seemed to be sulking.

"Splendid. I will immediately descend and let it be known that you will be guests for a while longer. Would you like to assist in the lab work?"

"Of course."

"Well, this *is* good news," Lydia said, lifting her manuscript and carrying it to the door. She stopped a moment. "I shall look forward to getting to know you all better." Her smile, though, was for Oliver alone. Then she was gone.

"I have asked to take dinner with you all to discuss our procedures more fully," Dr. Adamson said. "Until then . . ." He bowed with a trace of friendly formality and followed Lydia.

Once again in civilized atmosphere, Penton wore his butler's mask. "I have your clothes to see to, sir. Shall I draw a bath?"

"That would be fine, Penton," Oliver answered. He turned to Jennifer. "My goodness, Jenny. Things are working out well, aren't they?"

She was silent.

"Jennifer! Didn't you hear! They'll be working on a cure for us—Here, amid all this comfort!" He crouched by her chair. "And candy!"

Her head swept around. "And that woman!"

"What are you talking about?"

"Don't try to fool *me*, Oliver Dolan! I saw the way she looks at you. And you at *her*."

"I . . ." Oliver was about to deny it all, vow eternal hatred for Lydia Burthington. He had lied to Jennifer before, particularly when she inquired about Anziel Dubrelizy. However, after enjoying the company of a mature woman for several days, Oliver had begun to feel that the way to a worthwhile relationship was to be *truthful* without hedging. "I do find her interesting—don't you, Jenny? We had such a good conversation over dinner last night. You must admit, she's a very comely lady. I would not be male if I were not affected by attractive women, would I? That doesn't mean that anything has changed—"

"You admit it! You're tired of me! After all we've been through!"

Confused, Oliver blinked. "No, Jenny. I was just telling you the truth. Can't you accept—"

"How *dare* you! All those things you told me. What were they? Lies?"

Oliver stood, taking a deep breath. "No. No, of course not!"

"I don't *like* it here, Oliver. I want to go." She stomped to the window. Folding her arms tightly over her chest, she stared into the sunset through the window.

"But they're working for a *cure*, Jenny!"

She spun, pointing an accusing finger. "*You* want to stay so that you can be around that—that Squidia person. Admit it, Oliver! You don't care about me at all. You've just been *using* me all this time that I've *trusted* you! I'm so ashamed!"

"Jenny, be realistic. Just because I happen to be attracted to another woman. Well, I mean, it's *normal,* isn't it?"

"Normal! How can you say that! It's . . . it's perverted. You're *my* friend . . . my love. No one else, Oliver!"

It was *useless* to try to reason with her in her present state. It made him terribly anxious to see her so. He was happy when she was happy. He'd discovered that. He put his arm around her. "I'm sorry, Jenny."

"Don't touch me! Don't *ever* touch me again! I . . . I *hate* you. I *hate* you!"

Oliver recoiled from her assault. More than anything he wanted her approval. Somehow it seemed very important. But before he could speak, Jennifer had regained her breath.

"You don't know anything about real feeling, you cold fish! And I thought you were warm and loving and caring! I don't know what I ever saw in you, Oliver!"

"Jennifer! *Think,* will you? I haven't stopped caring. I certainly haven't said that I hate you or anything you should get upset over—"

"We're *through,* Oliver."

She slammed the door behind her.

The last of the sun was a red smear in the east, as the figure paced toward the castle gate, stepping lightly, long-coat and scarf flapping with the wind. By the gate stood a small shack with shingle roof and unpainted clapboard siding. Growls sounded from within.

From the folds of his coat, the man drew a paper-wrapped shank of raw meat, which he tossed into the shack. The man waited a moment while the beast noisily finished its repast.

"All right," he said, finally. "Come out. I need you a moment."

The basilisk slouched to the entrance, rooster head ominous in the shadows, lizard's tail slithering from sight.

"Left—*face!*"

With a cackling growl, the creature presented its right side to the man who played an electric torch over its hide until he found the tabs. He pushed both. A door sprung open, revealing a compartment in the creature's body. The man inserted a hand, extracted a telephone. After turning around to be sure that no one was watching, he brought the earpiece up to the side of his head and waited for a response.

"Hello?" he said. "Is your employer available yet? It's getting a bit cold, dearie. *Get* the blighter, would you? I'm freezing my tail out here."

He turned to the basilisk. "Good thing you and your dead companion didn't kill *them*. I have the feeling our guests might just be desired for other purposes."

The basilisk grunted in response.

The earpiece squawked, for a few seconds.

The man responded. "Yes. Yes, old bird. Good to hear from you . . . What? Could you speak up a bit? . . . Yes, absolutely. You got my message correctly. I'm glad I finally got through to you . . . Yes, they're still here. It would appear that they'll *be* here for a while longer . . . No, no—I assure you, everything is under control. They're in the best of health and spirits . . . Adamson and the Einstein are working out a way of killing off your disease . . . Yes! They've *both* got it . . . Who? Oliver Dolan, and the girl, Jennifer . . . Yes, I *thought* you'd be quite pleased at that bit of news. Um, Paler, I *trust* that you remember our deal . . . That's right—my cooperation here at HOPE, in return for a hands-off attitude toward us. We just want to be left alone . . . No. No, I suppose not . . . To your advantage, quite right. You *are* a civilized chap! . . . Your emissary will arrive in three days? Splendid. Then we can wash our hands of them. They're a bit too full of themselves for my taste. Smug, self-righteous twits . . . Well, of course Adamson wants to find out the cure. It's his nature, you know. You needn't get upset, it would take a very long time, and as you've said, they don't have a very long time, do they? Afterward, I'm sure it would be easy enough to . . . ah, lose the research on the matter—I know it's a touchy subject for you. Oh, by the way, you might send another basilisk. . . . A *jabberwock?* What would we want with a jabberwock?" . . . He sighed. "Oh, very well, whatever you say. Super! Till next time!"

He hung the receiver on the hook and placed the telephone back inside the basilisk. "All right, Fredrick, thank you *most* kindly. Back to sentry, dear chap. Perhaps we'll get you a companion very soon." He sent the beast off with an affectionate pat.

Mr. Sparrow pulled up the lapels of his longcoat and turned, smiling, as he noticed the homey lights glowing from the windows.

III: 3

OLIVER DOLAN sat in an overstuffed chair, so drunk he could barely move. "Women!" His voice was so slurred the word was barely comprehensible.

However, Caspar Penton, who'd matched his master glass for glass, had enough brandy in him to understand. "I shouldn't worry, sir."

"She said it's *over!* She told me herself! In those very words! Over!"

"Probably just wants a rise from you."

"She's ignored me all evening."

"You should be relieved. Take it while you can. You'll get an earful when she decides communication should begin again."

"You mean she didn't really mean our relationship is over?"

"Oh, I'm *quite* sure she meant every word. Women will tell you exactly what they feel. Brutally truthful about it. She'll be grouchy and grumpy awhile. Don't let it affect you. I'll tell you one thing about most women—they're as paradoxical as anything in God's nature. There's nothing they like better than to control a loved one. Yet as soon as they've whipped a fellow to the ground, they'll lose respect for him. He's not fulfilling his role, which is to keep *them* under control. Strange combatants, men and women. They contend fiercely for victory, yet, deep down, both would as soon surrender."

"I feel like I'm in a *maze!*" Despite his stupor, Oliver hurled himself to his feet, shaking a fist in frustration. "Why can't life be simpler?"

Pursing his lips, Penton studied his glass. "Who can say, Oliver?" He half-closed his eyes, relaxing. He was a changed man when within walls. A bundle of industry, he'd already mended the holes in Oliver's rough adventurer's clothes, strongly hinting that it might be wise to be measured for apparel more suitable to HOPE's genteel atmosphere. Clearly, Penton relished his role as manservant.

Oliver sighed. "I'm feeling a bit dizzy. It's stuffy in here. I need a breath of fresh air."

Lost in his own spiritous thoughts, Penton did not respond.

Oliver weaved by the table, found his way to the window-sill. With some effort, he managed to open the window. He stuck his head into the night. Immediately he noted the dark outline of Turner's van, which was parked in the courtyard. Someone who was staggering beneath the weight of a heavy burden seemed to be making for the van.

Unsure whether anything was amiss, Oliver merely observed the fellow's progress. The man reached the van and shoved a box through the van's rear entrance.

Oliver had locked that door himself. The only other key was with MacPherson. The box must be the Einstein!

He thought he'd convinced the man that God could wait. That they should rest for a while, *then* move on. Obviously, MacPherson had other ideas. That, or the Higher Authority buzzing messages into his ear had declined to wait.

"MacPherson!" he cried in a stage whisper. "What do you think you're doing?"

Startled, the man swung about and stared up at the lighted window. His sudden motion spooked the harnessed horses. "I must go. I cannot disobey His commands!"

"You can't take the Einstein!"

Angrily, MacPherson drew his sword. It flicked on brilliantly. *"Retros me, Satanas!"* He locked the doors, then walked to the driver's seat.

"I say, sir?" Penton inquired sleepily. "What's the ruckus?"

Trying to get a grip on sobriety, Oliver pointed a wavering finger toward the courtyard. "MacPherson! He's making off with the Einstein!"

"Good Lord. We must stop him, then!"

"How? He's got that sword of his, and he looks determined."

"No. No, that's no good. We're linked to MacPherson. Either *we* stop him . . . or go with him. He's left us with no choice."

"That Einstein is our hope! We've got to get it *back* here!"

"Sir, you're not thinking straight."

"Go out there. Talk to the man. But quietly. I'm going to get Jenny."

He flung himself through the door and staggered to Jenny's room.

Jennifer was propped comfortably in bed, reading Boethius. "Oh. Have you come to apologize?"

"Get dressed," he said. "MacPherson's stealing the Einstein. We might have to get out of here, fast."

She brightened. "I'd *like* that."

"It's a *wretched* turn of events, Jenny! That Einstein is our hope!"

"I see that I'll have you to myself again." She answered brightly. She was already pulling on her boots. She shrugged on her coat, then tossed her belongings into an open bag.

"Get *your* things!"

"No time!" He grabbed her arm, and they bolted into the corridor.

The hour was late and the hallways were clear. Somehow, Oliver managed not to knock anything over as they padded toward the courtyard. Adrenaline had chased some of the alcohol from his system, but enough remained that his gait was noticeably unsteady.

The main door, a large oaken affair with brass studs and bolts, stood ajar. Jennifer pushed it open, and its hinges complained loudly.

"Shh!" Oliver said. "If we rouse—" He noticed Caspar Penton lying face down in the mud some feet into the yard. The van was making for the gate.

Oliver scampered over and pulled the man up. Water and blood covered his face, but he was still breathing. MacPherson had obviously ended their discussion with a blow.

"Are you all right, man?"

"My head! My *nose!*"

"Still there. Can you stand?"

"I . . . I think so." With Oliver and Jennifer supporting him along, they pursued MacPherson.

"He's got to get through the gate first!" Oliver said.

A cackling roar resounded through the night.

"Not to mention the basilisk," Penton noted.

Only partially covered by clouds, both moons outlined the figure of the basilisk upright before the approaching van. It appeared fully ready for battle, claws held high. Its screeches would surely rouse the populace soon.

"*MacPherson!* Stop! You're making a terrible mistake!"

The horses halted before the nightcreature, and MacPherson ignited his sword and hurled himself at the beast. The weapon flashed in mid-flight and struck downward to sever the left wing. The member fell to the ground, flapping.

The basilisk howled, then backed, raising its claws and coiling its serpentine tail. MacPherson swiftly swung again, his blade slicing upward. The creature's torso was cleaved from abdomen to neck and the contents of its interior—biological and mechanical—spilled. The beast was given only a moment to shudder and reel before a final stroke removed head from neck.

MacPherson advanced to the gate and began to struggle with the great bolt. By this time, Oliver and the others had caught up with him. Oliver dropped Penton's arm and ran to confront MacPherson.

"Are you insane! I told you we have to stay here!" He turned and gazed at the fallen basilisk. "I want you to turn the van around and return the Einstein!"

Not reacting at first to Oliver's demands, MacPherson pushed back the wooden bolt, then forced the gates open wide enough to allow passage of the van. When he turned to confront Oliver, his eyes seemed lit from within.

He raised his sword, switched it on.

Oliver flinched. "MacPherson! What's *wrong* with you?"

Angry cries rang out from behind and the courtyard lights switched on.

MacPherson checked himself mid-blow. His features contorted an instant, then became stern once more. "Get in the van."

Oliver realized there was no other recourse. Having been caught red-handed "stealing" the Einstein, if they stayed at HOPE they might well be shot. MacPherson was already striding resolutely to the driver's seat of the van.

Oliver spun around, said, "Well, you heard him."

Jennifer and Penton were already at the van, Penton hobbling unaided behind Jennifer, who was struggling with the van's back door. Oliver unlocked it, and Jennifer and Penton entered. But before Oliver could climb in a rifle shot pinged off a stone by his foot and another ricocheted from the nearby wall. Though the van was but a yard away, it had already begun to move.

"Slow *down!*" Jennifer yelled. The wild man disregarded her. His whip snapped, driving the horses faster. Oliver dashed frantically after them as the van passed under the Norman arch into the night.

"Stop!" an angry voice cried behind them amid the general confusion and bustle of the pursuing party. "Stop, thieves!"

"Oliver! *Run!*" Jennifer cried.

"Here, sir!" Penton switched on the interior light of the van so that Oliver could see his destination.

"No! Don't do that—" If Oliver could see it, then most certainly the pursuers could as well.

An explosion lit the night, and something stung Oliver's backside and legs. He cried out, but the pain did succeed in driving him to the frenzy needed to catch the van.

A hand caught his. Pulled into the van, he lay on the floor, gasping. "Turn out the bloody light!"

Penton obeyed. Then he shut the door.

Penton switched the light back on.

"Oliver," Jennifer said. "You've been hit!"

"I wouldn't have known," Oliver replied through gritted teeth.

"Just pellets," Penton said, examining the wounds while Jennifer pretended to look away. "Kissed by a shotgun once myself, while a corporal in the Penzance brigade. Nothing serious. Hurt like hell extracting the bastards, though."

"Oh, Penton! We had exactly what we needed. Why don't things ever work out right?"

Jennifer, who'd been stroking his hair, halted her ministrations. "You've got that mechanical box there. You've got me. What more do you want?"

"Oh God, spare me," Oliver said. "Explain it to her, would you, Penton?"

"I think what the master means, Miss Eden, is that certain laboratory conditions are necessary if one is to utilize the Einstein properly. To say nothing of Dr. Adamson's help. Our early departure leaves us in a bit of a fix. We're back on that madman's journey now. Who knows what awaits?

"There's nothing to do now but wait until old MacPherson stops so that we can talk to him," Penton continued. "Meantime, we should get those pellets from you. Fortunately, we've Turner's medical equipment. Tweezers and scalpel should be sufficient for our purposes. Some alcohol—"

"Definitely!" Oliver whimpered.

"Um, I meant *medicinal* alcohol to prevent infection, Oliver."

"Well, there's plenty of the other stuff, too!" Oliver said.

Jennifer leaned over him. "Oliver, I'm sorry this happened, I truly am."

Oliver remained sullenly silent.

Her voice became pouty. "Aren't you going to talk to me, Oliver?"

Oliver tried to focus on the rattling and bumps of the van as it progressed toward wherever.

"You really liked her, didn't you? Better than me, Oliver?"

He sighed away his pent-up fury. No sense in making things worse. "No, Jenny. It was all inside your head."

"I'm sorry, Oliver."

Sure she was. They were both fairly sorry creatures. Still . . .

"Things will be better, Oliver, I promise. You'll see. Everything will turn out just fine." Her voice regained its former childlike enthusiasm. She stroked his head again. He liked it.

Penton rattled about in the medical drawer. He pulled out the necessary tools. He handed a bottle of malt whiskey to Jennifer. "You may administer the general anesthetic to the patient."

Jennifer did just that, murmuring inanely as he sipped from the bottle.

He looked into her eyes. Genuine love radiated from them. His spirits greatly improved.

Soon he had to doff his breeches once again, and Jennifer held his head in her lap, cooing to him softly. At first he felt only a very little pain.

"Dear Oliver," Jennifer said. "Dear, dear Oliver!"

"Well, *dear* sir," Penton said, "this next one's deep."

Then it began to hurt. Badly.

Jennifer leaned over to whisper: "You need this." Suddenly, her thumb was in his mouth.

Somehow, she had contrived to prick it. Blood trickled into Oliver's mouth, warmly, sweetly.

The pain and the alcohol had driven all reason from him. As he swallowed the blood, warmth, tranquility, and complete trust filled his body, vanquishing the pain of Penton's surgical enterprise. His being seemed to extend from his own body through Jennifer's thumb, through her arm and into her mind, where her love washed over him, like a wave of warm water.

THE EINSTEIN'S LIGHTS were blinking randomly, causing the machine to glitter like a cubist's Christmas tree.

"Well, it appears the converter is working properly," Oliver said, indicating a readout embedded in its side. "Although I don't want to run it from the van's batteries too long."

"Doesn't the Einstein have its own batteries?"

"Certainly, Penton, but I'd rather not drain those. I think it needs residual power at all times to keep operational. But then, that's one of the many questions we must ask it." He turned and glared at the gaunt man beside him. "True, MacPherson?"

"I told you! The machine will bear me out. Follow the words of the Lord, and your path will be made clear."

"No sugar for the tea, I'm afraid," Jennifer stated, happily measuring spoons of dried leaf for the pot.

Oliver grunted, kneeling by the machine, trying to remember the proper combination of switches to summon its voice.

When he awoke that morning, the van was motionless. His rear had hurt like blazes. A hangover split his head. However, the need to confront MacPherson had caused him to shoulder aside his personal difficulties.

MacPherson had parked the van well within a copse of trees. Oliver found him sitting beside a tree trunk, half asleep, still clutching his sword. The dead leaves had rustled under Oliver's feet as he approached and MacPherson immediately jumped to his feet, ready.

"I just want an explanation."

MacPherson nodded his head, lowering his sword. "The man Sparrow was betraying us." MacPherson strode to the driver's seat and retrieved something covered with gore. "I cut this Devil's device from the beast—God tells me it's a communications machine. I heard him. He spoke with the Vampire Lord, our enemy, calling him 'Paler.' Paler was supposed to send forces to waylay us. I notified my God. He ordered me to take the box immediately."

"What about us?" Oliver said, doubt filling his voice. "Your God was just going to abandon us?"

For the first time in Oliver's experience, MacPherson smiled. "He told me you would never believe me. You were too involved there, too settled. But, I made sure that you were aware of my departure, assuming that you would join me."

"A bloody close thing! But you're right. I wouldn't have believed you, and I'm not sure I do now."

"The answers are in the machine," MacPherson said. "Ask it."

So Oliver washed up, breakfasted with the others on their dwindling supplies, then unwrapped the stolen merchandise.

"I perceive I have been kidnapped."

"You deduce most logically," Oliver said.

"That is my function. In light of my importance to the community of HOPE, I trust there is good reason for this action. Was it a violent kidnapping?"

"No one was hurt except the basilisk guarding the gate."

"A very small loss. According to my memory, we have never much liked basilisks."

"Nor werewolves, or gryphons or any other nightcreatures," Penton observed dryly.

"Quite."

Although the machine sounded like the late Geoffrey Turner, Oliver began to realize he could never *feel* about the machine in the same way. Though it obviously had most of Turner's memory, his thought patterns, and voice, it did not have his humanity. Quite simply, it wasn't *alive*.

"Now, Einstein—" Oliver began.

"Please. Turner. Geoffrey Turner."

"Yes. Mr. Turner. You see, Miss Eden, Mr. Penton, and I did not favor your kidnapping. That was perpetrated by Mr. MacPherson. Circumstances forced us to accompany you. As you know, we need your valuable intelligence and analytical capabilities to develop a serum that will cure Miss Eden and myself."

"I aided in determining the nature of your disease. Yes, I am cognizant of these things. It is natural that you be concerned with my well-being."

"We'd very much like to proceed upon our medical course with Dr. Adamson, but Mr. MacPherson claims at least one traitor exists among the members of HOPE. Exactly *why* this meant he should stash you in the van and take off for parts unknown is not entirely clear to us."

Oliver glared unhappily at MacPherson. "He claims that you will be able to assure us of the wisdom of his actions."

"Excuse me," MacPherson said to the machine. "I have . . . studied you. You seem of good intent. God Himself ordered that you be stolen and taken—" He hesitated and doubt played momentarily on his features. *"Where,* He has not yet specified."

"You realize, Mr. MacPherson, that I am an atheist. I do not believe in God. Therefore, if indeed you have been called by something or someone, it is, in my judgment, most certainly not God."

MacPherson bridled, but contained his anger. "Please. Let me continue. My master said that certain information would make you capable of understanding why I was commanded to take you, and where we should take you."

"A tall order, Mr. MacPherson. A traitor among HOPE? It seems unlikely. What evidence do you have?"

MacPherson recounted his spying activities. Sparrow's conversation with the Vampire Lord was related almost verbatim.

"Most curious," the machine said. "It would appear that Sparrow is not necessarily betraying HOPE, but rather attempting to maintain the status quo. From previous information, it is easily recognizable that this Paler is attempting to assume a position of greater power upon Styx. I encountered Mr. Paler perhaps a century and a half ago—or rather, Geoffrey Turner Prime did. Very clever chap. Perhaps even too human for his own good. Too big for his britches, that chap."

"So. This Vlad Paler and the Vampire Lord are one and the same?" Penton interrupted. "Namely, the developer of this genetic disease?"

"Yes, indeed, Mr. Penton. As I recall, I ran into a test colony of the stuff on rather a disturbing adventure. Satan had every member destroyed. He didn't feel he had sufficient control. Particularly after his problems with Mr. Paler's rebellion." Lights flashed for a moment. "You say, Mr. MacPherson, that you were ordered to extract the device that you observed Mr. Sparrow utilizing to communicate with Mr. Paler. Would you please place it before my scanner?"

MacPherson dashed to the van and immediately returned with the grisly item.

"By the lights, if you please," the machine ordered. Concentric circles of green and blue light flashed along the right side of the yard-wide cube.

MacPherson held the mechanism within a white beam.

"Interesting," the machine said finally. "I have determined the frequency—we can ring Mr. Paler anytime."

"What?" Oliver said, disbelievingly.

"You wish to determine the exact nature of our nemesis, do you not? What better way than by direct communication? As I recall, Vlad Paler has the gift of gab. He may well let things slip that, though they may not assist us, will provide a larger picture of the situation. I am rather in the dark on that subject."

"Do you need to attach the—um, telephone to yourself in any way?" Penton asked.

"No. I have the faculties to duplicate its function. Now, if you all just drink your tea, by the time you have finished I will have raised Mr. Paler."

It seemed a very few minutes before the group's silent musings were interrupted by the Einstein. "I have raised him."

"An appropriate verb, that."

"I suggest that you do not anger him, Mr. Penton, if you care to talk with him for any period of time. He can always cut you off if the conversation displeases him. I will channel the voice through speakers. Do not mention me. Claim to be utilizing the communication system you removed from the basilisk."

"Hello?" a cultured voice asked. "Who is this? Sparrow. That you, chap? What's happened?"

Penton gestured for Oliver to speak.

"You are the creature known as Vlad Paler?" Oliver asked, nervously.

Suspicion crept into the voice. "I am Vlad, Lord Paler, yes. Who is this? This is Sparrow's—oh dear. Something is wrong, isn't it? Dear Sparrow has fouled his nest."

"My name is Oliver Dolan."

"My goodness! Why, what a terrific pleasure. Finally, to speak to one of my liberators." Static obscured the voice briefly, then disappeared. "—must tell me how you came to locate this communications unit. You *are* resourceful, Mr. Dolan!"

"We observed Mr. Sparrow communicating with you via the basilisk. Naturally we thought it best to depart immediately."

"What?" The voice seemed filled with an odd good humor. "You hauled the basilisk along with you?"

"No. I'm afraid he's dead."

"Ah ha! The work of your Mr. MacPherson, no doubt. Wonderful piece of work, that, from all accounts. Is he listening?"

"Aye, ye black spawn of Satan. Neither I nor my Lord shall rest till ye be dead and buried in Hell!"

Penton waved his hands wildly at MacPherson.

"My goodness. The man's as hot as his sword! Doesn't sound as if it's worth bargaining with you chaps!"

"Bargaining?" Oliver said. "We don't even know what you're doing, who you really are. What do you have to bargain with us about?"

"Yet you have been behaving *most* reprehensibly, destroying the citizens of my new race. Cold-blooded murderers—that's what you *seem* to be. Particularly you, Mr. MacPherson. Merely because my poor vampires are *different* from you, you want to slash them up!"

MacPherson was speechless with anger, but Oliver retained control of his tongue. "And what do you think your vampires do? We know about you, Paler. You control the victims of this disease, don't you? They're your slaves, after they're killed!"

"Slaves? Oh my, no! They are of the New Order. I admit, they follow my orders occasionally. But they're not killers. *They're* not murderers!"

Oliver calmed down. "Very well. What are they? Tell us about yourself. We're talking now. We may *well* be able to bargain. At least we'll all know where we stand."

"Excellent, Mr. Dolan. We are both intelligent, civilized beings. Why must we be enemies? I admit to great anger at your activities. But then, with your background one can understand your violent proclivities, your distrust of the creatures created by Hedley Nicholas. As well you know, Mr. Dolan, Satan is dead, but please do not regard me as Satan's successor. I do not suffer his delusions, nor am I any less sane than yourself."

"Well then, what are you trying to do?"

"I shall do my best. Quite simply, I, Vlad, Lord Paler, am a creature of vision. I have no desire for absolute power, I wish merely to make this world—interesting. To take it a step forward in the evolution of consciousness. I wish to create a good, just world. I know well the pitiful history of mankind—from which we are all derived—a sorry sequence of events! I am merely experimenting, dear boy! My vampires, alas, are imperfect. But change is possible. What is the alternative? Have you any idea of the number and kinds of nations that are being formed as we speak, the wars that are about to begin? *Mankind* loves war, not I. I must confess—I desire *some* power, but only enough to implement my visions. Please. Whatever you think of me, do not view me as a monomaniac who lusts after absolute power.

"What do I wish? Well, I'd like you to visit me, if you can. I learned from Mr. Sparrow that . . . oh dear, what is her name. Oh, yes. That Miss Eden is a candidate for my order, and that you wish her to revert to her former state. I can arrange that easily! I confess, though, that the origins of Mr. MacPherson are a mystery to me. I should like to talk to him, perhaps come to peace."

"Never!" MacPherson cried. "Never will I negotiate with a servant of the Devil!"

"Gracious! Chap's a bit loony, don't you think, Mr. Dolan? And you're following *his* orders! I trust you'll realize the benefits of my suggestions and visit me in my manse. By my reckoning, the journey would take only a month, if you'll board a ferry or two. I'm not that far away."

"You're very persuasive, Vlad Paler," Oliver said calmly. "Yet I have seen your vampires, and their works. In them I see nothing but evil."

"Oh dear, you simply can't get yourself out of that mindset, can you, Mr. Dolan? Good. Evil. And you say my . . . um, shall we say the New Order is *evil*, when actually . . . well, actually they're simply *different!*"

"All they want to do is drain the rest of us, make us like them, under your command!"

"Oh, that's not so bad, I assure you! Dear, dear Oliver! I like you already. From what Mr. Sparrow says, you and Mr. Penton and Miss Eden are delightful people. Do come and visit me. Oliver, my boy! This is your chance! I know you've a vision, too! I'm open to suggestion. Please remember, it's hard to say when everything will change!"

"What do you mean?" Oliver asked, voice softening.

"Why, when the current Earth civilization comes to visit again. They know all about us now, don't they? You realize that as well as I. I know that you want to prepare the populace of this planet for that. Well, that can certainly be fitted in with my hopes!"

"And if we don't? If we continue to oppose you?"

"Well, you'll be disposed of. Regretfully. Please, come and visit me. Things will be made clear."

Oliver glanced at Penton, who shrugged. Jennifer seemed fascinated by the sound of the man's voice. She used the conversation's lull to speak up herself.

"Mr. Paler. I do not remember my experience with vampires as being particularly pleasant."

"I admit there are yet bugs in the system. The poor dears cherish certain preconceptions about vampirism. You know. Coffins. Things like that. But as soon as I work it out, things will change. I promise!"

"He sounds such a nice man," Jennifer said.

"You forget, Miss Jennifer. He's not a man."

"Not a man, Penton? Oh, how can you *say* that. Not a man! Was your Mr. Turner a man, Oliver? So, what do you say? We have much to offer one another, not the least of which is good fellowship."

MacPherson stepped smartly to Oliver's side and whispered in his ear: "Beware the wiles of the Devil, Oliver Dolan." His voice softened entreatingly. "Please. Trust me, and trust the Lord God."

"Paler!" Oliver said, rubbing his cheek thoughtfully. "I admit I would like to visit you. First, let us finish this quest which we have started upon."

"You refuse my invitation! You have just been . . . *using* this conversation, haven't you, you wretch, to learn about me."

"I thought that was clear from the beginning," Oliver replied.

"Oliver Dolan," Vlad Paler said. "You will regret your birth." With a sizzle, the communication link severed.

"Vindictive chap, what?" Penton said.

MacPherson was actually smiling broadly. "The Devil cannot bear to be mocked."

"I don't think anyone likes that much," Oliver observed. "Now. Mr. Ein—um, Mr. Turner. Mr. MacPherson claims that you can clear things up."

"I will answer any question I can."

"Very well. Although he doesn't believe it, there is a radio implant near Mr. MacPherson's left ear. Can you detect that?"

"Yes. It is a Binder Machazoid, MK 903A. Quite sophisticated. One of Satan's standard cyborg communication implants. It is the only purely mechanical aspect of Mr.

MacPherson. Curious, though. His skeletal network *has* been strengthened with duralloy and his muscular system augmented."

MacPherson's eyes were wide with surprise.

"I checked the map this morning, Mr. Turner. With your knowledge of geography and this information about Mr. MacPherson's . . . shall we say, *additions,* where would you deduce that we are going to if we continue our present southwesterly heading?"

"That is simple. The nexus of this world's former computer system."

Oliver smiled. "I thought so. Computer Mountain, Geoffrey Turner called it."

The Einstein said, "And Hedley Nicholas called it Hell."

Night descended like a black shroud.

Jerkin hobbled along, eyes eagerly searching the horizon for the lights of a community. None, however, were in evidence. Only straggly trees and clumps of gorse showed on the rolling moors.

He cursed under his misting breath, then wound his cloak tighter. Supplies were getting low. If he didn't find a place to kip, bloody soon, he'd get stiff as the trees that leaned all about him like old grave markers.

Even walking to HOPE with that crazed bunch had been better than fruitless foraging in the winter forest. There'd been the warm fires and hot food in his belly at night. Not to mention that pretty piece Jennifer to rest his eyes on. What a bizarre group! Jerkin half-believed in God most times; he even prayed when he was scared. But that MacPherson bloke was off his bean. Still, even his long-winded sermons were more comforting than the cry of the timber wolf out here, the scream of the icy wind.

And that Dolan bloke—just didn't know how to handle women!

Jerkin grinned with great self-satisfaction. *He* knew how to handle women. His thoughts sank into a brief reverie on the subject.

The sun had fully set. What remained of its light was squeezed flat along the horizon, flesh pink running to blood red. Stars slowly ignited in their black bed, as Athena rose in the cloudy north.

Like being in some giant dead church, Jerkin thought as he stumped along methodically. First thing *he* was going to do when he reached a community was to find a decent job.

Maybe go to a real church. Let the rosy-cheeked reverends do the thinking for him. On his own, he'd fouled his life up bad, and—

Something moved in the dark forest. A dark form bobbed above the trees. Jerkin froze. Bastards hadn't given him any weapons. A crack sounded. *A loud* crack. Not a twig snapping, but a whole bloody tree. He dropped low, started to slink for cover.

Before he could reach the trees, however, a huge thing bounded pall-mall through a break in the trees like a beast fleeing the jaws of Hell itself. With astonishing speed it reached him and stopped alongside.

Jerkin moaned, too petrified with fear to move.

A claw carefully picked at his coat, scratching his shoulder beneath not at all. It hoisted him ten feet in the air. Instinctively, Jerkin struggled, but to absolutely no avail.

Baleful eyes stared at the captive. "Sorry 'bout this, mate. Orders." The creature beckoned with its free paw to a nondescript figure nonchalantly picking its way through the frigid undergrowth, but Jerkin was too scared to notice.

Suddenly, the creature's chest seemed to explode with light. Dazzled, Jerkin stilled his struggle. He was fascinated by the twirling light patterns. Jerkin never even noticed the newcomer's red eyes though he certainly came close enough.

Marcus Sparrow, unable to sleep, sat in his room smoking furiously. Things were not going well. Not at all.

As head of security, much of the blame for the loss of Geoffrey Turner's Einstein had been heaped on his shoulders. If the investigation delved too deeply, his fellows might even discover his connection with Vlad Paler. He'd only consorted with the Vampire Lord for the sake of the community! How dreadfully ironic.

A cloud of bluish cigarette smoke hung roiling above the chair, a reflection of his thoughts. An oval clock ticked on the mantelpiece above the dead gray ashes of the fireplace. Sparrow sat brooding, trying to decide what was to be done. If he could only recover that Einstein!

A bell tinkled: the doorbell was connected to the front gate. It did not ring often. It was Sparrow's duty to answer the door at night. Still, the sound startled him.

The bell rang again, insistently.

Dolan and his party had fled two nights before. Could they be returning? Highly doubtful, that; yet hope stirred in Sparrow as he dashed down steps and across the yard to answer the ring.

Reaching the gate, he jerked open the slot-door, peered through the bars.

Just a few feet from the portcullis stood a dark figure.

"Who is it?" Sparrow demanded through chattering teeth.

"It's Jerkin, Sparrow."

"Jerkin! Good Lord, we booted you with orders never to return!"

"Found meself an employer, Mr. Sparrow. Friend of yours. Sent me to talk to you. Name of Vlad Paler. Ring a bell, chum?"

"Paler? How did—"

"Just open the door. Cold here. Mr. Paler says to tell you he can help you get back what you lost."

"The Einstein! Of course!" Sparrow answered enthusiastically. Paler might be able to bail him out. He'd become something of a pariah these past two days. "Just a moment." He unlatched the gate and hauled it open. "Welcome," he said brightly.

Jerkin paced in briskly, then his fist flew and Sparrow was sprawled on the stones, Jerkin atop him, a knee planted squarely on his chest.

"Good Heavens, man. What—"

"Oh vigilant Sparrow! You not only let Dolan and company kill my dear basilisks, you allowed Dolan *et alia* to depart before I could deal with them. It is time to take the matter into my own hands. Perhaps the Holy Order to Preserve the Empire, as fascinating as it is, is too much a wild card. Too, I can always use new recruits." Jerkin laughed deliciously.

Sparrow opened his mouth, but before he could cry out, a wad of cloth was stuffed into it.

"There," Jerkin said. "Now, dear Sparrow. All your worries will soon be over. Just lie very still for the minimum of pain. There's a good chap!"

Sharp fangs glinted from Jerkin's mouth as they descended toward Sparrow's neck.

A FAMILIAR DESTINATION AHEAD, Oliver Dolan was able to collect his thoughts, strengthen his resolve. Things were making marginal sense again; the quest had clear purpose once more. However, the opposition was clear now as well. Plainly, Vlad Paler was aware of approximately where they were and, perhaps, where they were going. Haste seemed necessary. At the next community they sold the horses, charged their batteries to optimum power, and increased their speed.

A hint of spring warmth had entered the air, and travel became less arduous, certainly less damp. According to their calculations, at their travel rate it would require almost two weeks to reach Computer Mountain.

The first week passed without significant incident.

To conserve power, the Einstein was fully activated only occasionally, to consult about the route or how to effect minor repairs to the van's equipment. Oliver would have liked to speak with it for longer, drawing upon Geoffrey Turner's experiences during his five centuries on Styx. That would probably have to wait until the end of their journey.

As to exactly what was transpiring, Penton had a theory he shared only with Oliver. Evidently, the computer system that had once ruled Styx still functioned to some degree, perhaps automatically producing more nightcreatures. Perceiving the threat to the status quo posed by Vlad Paler, it was working to balance the situation. Still, something vital was missing. The only way to discover what that was, as well as the actual cure for the disease, lay in achieving entrance to the Computer Nexus.

Meantime, Jennifer took it upon herself to keep the van, interior and exterior, straight and tidy. She seemed blissfully unaware of the importance of their journey. Her displeasure was evident only when Oliver somehow indicated opposition to her wishes. Otherwise, she was positively smug. Her head was full of plans for the life she and Oliver would lead once this unfortunate business was tidied up. Indeed, in her mind's eye she had her trousseau selected, the decor of their cottage picked, and its arrangement well thought out; their children had been named. Jennifer determined that Oliver *must* settle down to study his role as Viscount Dolan so as to insure the security of their offspring. To keep the peace among their small company, Oliver generally humored Jennifer, though he had severe doubts about the possibility of *any* long-term future for them, much less a cozy marriage.

Once, alone with Penton—a precious time indeed, for Jennifer was still jealous of their friendship—Oliver had asked: "How can she talk about these things? We're close to death from plague! Maybe things worse than death! She should be thinking about . . . I don't know—about why things are the way they are on this world, in this Universe. About God and life and death. Not about *babies,* for goodness sake!"

"Dear fellow!" Penton said. "You've accidentally hit her baby-machine button. Just part of the security fabric she wishes to weave for herself."

"But she hasn't even asked me about anything! She just assumes!"

"She assumes that you assume similarly, sir. After all it *is* the thing to do, the thing that's been programmed into you, into *her* by society."

Oliver put his hands to his face. "But dammit! I'm not a machine! I'm not a machine and neither should she be!"

"Sir, you must realize that creations of man are always reflections of himself."

"No. I can't accept that! People are human. When they act like machines, it's wrong. We're more than that, we have to be!"

"Sir, I disagree only with your phrasing. Perhaps you should say: People are machines, and when they act like humans, it's *right.*"

And so, during a lull of their journey, Oliver came to realize that he had been enlisted in a private war, one in which there were no victors and no enemies.

He wondered about Penton's pronouncement, that the creations of men are the reflections of their own inner working.

Such thoughts pained him. In the end, he found comfort against them in Jennifer's arms, where introspection had no place.

Wintry moors gave way to fields and forests, edged with distant mountains on one side, the flatness of a sea on the other. Clouds no longer had an ominous quality.

As he slogged along, Darkwing welcomed the spring. Lately, he'd grown weary of dark things. Even his own name no longer had the nasty ring to it he'd always savored so much, the flash of deviltry that he had once thought defined him. *No,* he thought glumly as he trudged up a hill, his wings flopping forlornly about, *things just don't make sense anymore, not the way they used to.* Now all he had was Paler's promise that normal life—whatever *that* was these days—would be restored to him.

Darkwing had nothing against Dolan or his party. Goodness, he'd had nothing against that Jerkin fellow that Paler had him chase after for conversion.

"They're headed for the Mountain!" Paler had said. "Don't you understand, this is more important than I'd thought it would be! You're the only thing I have to watch them, to prevent them from doing something I don't want. *Kill* them, if necessary. Now get moving, or I'll be forced to override your sorry excuse for a brain, you slothful beast!"

Darkwing had never heard Lord Paler so dreadfully upset. Although it was doubtful that Paler would devote time to animating the jabberwock himself, he had other methods to prod the beast onward, jabs of interior pain and, of course, the ultimate threat, that wonderful explosive device.

Darkwing did not argue. He wearily continued the obsessed vampire's mission. And that was what really rankled —after the dissolution of Satan's power—and even on the sly, before that—he'd been his own jabberwock. Now he was at the mercy of a mean-hearted controller, a manipulator with about as much interest in Darkwing's actual welfare as that rock on top of this rise. If he ever got out of this, it was for certain he'd extract a great deal of revenge, if that was remotely possible.

He crested the hill and gazed into the next valley. Below lay one of the paved roadways that crisscrossed Styx. Silently moving along the road at a good clip was a horseless van. Darkwing swiftly ducked behind the large boulder at the hilltop. Paler would raise hell if he were spotted.

Quickly, the jabberwock fumbled with the transmission controls. He signaled extreme emergency.

Evidently, Paler was close to his transmission desk. His voice crackled immediately, followed by his image. "Yes! What is it, old chum?"

"Just down in the valley. A van. Self-powered, just as you described."

"Where? Let me see, immediately!"

The jabberwock sidled around to provide Paler a view of the van and the small roostertail of dust behind it. Two riders sat outside the front seat. Obviously at least one person had to be inside, directing it.

"Hit magnification eight-by, would you, Darkwing? There's a good lad . . . Appears to be Oliver Dolan and the young lady. See if we can eavesdrop on them. Just punch the second button marked P and cup your ears."

The jabberwock obeyed.

". . . and what do you think about the blue for Osgood's bedroom, Oliver? I've always favored blue, myself. Particularly robin's-egg blue."

"Osgood?"

"Oliver! Our second son, of course! How *could* you have forgotten?"

"Sorry, but I have trouble keeping the children's names in mind."

"Well, they won't be imaginary for long. Now, as I was saying, I want Osgood to be a doctor. What kind of decorations, paintings, wallpaper do you think would mold his mind toward that disposition?"

A sigh. "Anatomical diagrams of dissected animals?"

"Oliver! That's nothing to put in a child's room."

"I was jesting, dear."

"I think you should be more serious about this. After all, the family *is* the cornerstone of decent society."

Vlad Paler chuckled. "She's got the disease, all right." His voice assumed a more serious tone. "By my estimation, they will arrive at the Mountain in another four days."

"You don't want me to destroy them yet?" Relief swept through Darkwing.

"No. I've tried to enter the Mountain, even mounted an expeditionary force. I had no success. I want to observe them—perhaps we'll find a way in. Besides, there are things I wish to discover that I'll never find out if you destroy them."

"What do you wish me to do?"

A pause. "Something infinitely more subtle, my dear Darkwing. It will thoroughly disgust you, I'm sure."

Only two more days to go.

Bone weary, Oliver prepared for his watch. The fire blazed before him, there now more for light than warmth. Still, there was a slight nip to the air. Oliver had draped a woolen blanket over his shoulders, and was sipping a mug of steaming tea.

MacPherson, more fired up than was usual even for him, had wanted to drive through the night using the headlights. But the others were tired and cranky from the long drive, particularly Jennifer. Besides, the headlights were a real drain on the battery.

There had been no signs of interference from Paler. In fact, the countryside was practically deserted. According to the Einstein, any communities that had been built so close to Nicholas's lair were soon and easily overrun by his forces. The nightcreature dens had either been deserted by their denizens after Satan's demise or, more likely, become totally dependent because so close to the control. Hence, when Satan had died, they'd died as well.

Leaves stirred behind him.

He turned. Jennifer shuffled toward him. She plopped down beside him, arms crossed, wearing a disgruntled expression.

Oliver tossed a twig into the fire. "What's wrong with you?"

"Nothing."

"Very well. You probably can't sleep. Did you drink too much tea today, as usual?"

"None of your business."

"So what's wrong then. You've been sulking since noon."

She turned her head away and stared into the darkness.

Oliver sighed. He glanced back at the van to be sure neither MacPherson nor Penton had roused, then he rolled back his right sleeve. Red marks abounded. He drew a long needle from his pocket and prepared to sterilize it in the fire.

"Do you think that's what I want?" Her voice was hurt.

"You're in a bad mood. I assumed—"

"Well, you're wrong. I don't need it. And don't think you're going to get any from me, either."

"I didn't ask for any. As a matter of fact, I'd just as soon be alone. What we have is fine, Jenny, but a person needs some solitude once in a while. Can't you understand that? You can't just poke about in a person's head at your whim."

"That's why you've been so resentful, so . . . so cold to me today! You're tired of me. If you want to know, you're what's wrong, Oliver. You!"

147

"Look. Can't I be a little moody, too? I've been under a lot of pressure lately."

"From me? Is that what you're saying? You're just plain tired of me, aren't you? I don't understand you at all."

With an exasperated sigh, he rolled down his sleeve. Funny. This sounded exactly like the argument they'd had about three days earlier. Well, last time, he had acquiesced, fighting off her displeasure by swearing eternal devotion. Well, she was going to have more than she could handle tonight. "I never asked you to understand me! A *home? Children?* A fire in the hearth? Milk and cookies? Pipe dreams, Jennifer. Chances are we won't come out of this alive, and *you're* making plans. Like you bloody *own* me or something. I'm the actor you've selected for the play you've got all plotted. Let's just take comfort in one another *now.* Make allowances. Give as well as take. Just *be!*"

"You mean you don't want to get married?" She seemed honestly shocked.

"Have I ever said anything about it? Have I *asked* you?"

"But . . . we're *supposed* to be together. Always. Jennifer and Oliver. It's . . . it's supposed to be that way. We're . . . part of one being, Oliver." Her eyes were tearing.

"Let me find out what it means to me first."

"Don't you love me, Oliver?"

"I guess so."

"You guess so! When you're in love, you don't doubt it for a minute!"

"Who told you that? Your goddamned father?" He mimicked another voice, low and deep. "Yes, dear child, and when you grow up to be a wonderful young lady you'll meet Prince Charming, who'll look just like Daddy, treat you nice like Daddy, tell you what to do like Daddy, paddle your little behind when you're naughty just like Daddy. You'll live happily ever after with your surrogate Daddy, just like it's supposed to be." He shook his head sadly. "Jennifer, start thinking for yourself, please!"

"I do!"

"You think you do."

A moment of leaden silence hung in the air. A fissure had suddenly opened between them. Oliver took one breath, two. He could not read her. The blond head was buried in updrawn knees. He calmed, then tried to play down the argument. "Jennifer, you have to understand. We're *both* under pressure. Maybe—maybe that's why I'm the way I've been to you. Maybe that's why you've been so cloying."

"Cloying. Love is cloying?"

"Why don't we just drop it, okay? We're both tired. We can talk about it tomorrow. That's best, don't you think?" He leaned over to pat her shoulder affectionately.

She recoiled, glaring at him in contempt. "Don't touch me! I hate you!" she cried. "I *hate* you." Her fury mounting, Jennifer launched herself. Her fingernails raked across his cheek. She began pounding him with tiny fists, kicking him and snarling, "I hate you, I hate you, I hate you!"

Stunned into total bemusement for a moment, Oliver let the blows rain without defense. But he didn't want her to wake up MacPherson and Penton. That would be dreadfully embarrassing. So he grabbed her wrists. Not judging his own force properly, he accidentally threw her to the ground. "Now settle down!"

She came up with leaves and twigs in her hair. She sobbed.

Oliver cursed and turned his back on her.

He heard her snivel once. With a swoosh of her clothing, she began to run. The light stamping of her feet disappeared into the shrubs that surrounded the clearing.

For a moment, he felt a twinge of fear. He almost hopped up and went after her. She might not be safe out there.

It took every bit of his willpower to force himself to stay still, not go after her.

She'll be okay, he told himself. She'd pout and sulk for a while, get frightened and come creeping back, and he'd win for once. He'd win this little battle, and it was as much for her sake as his that he wasn't going after her. Wasn't it?

Bloody right!

Jennifer could go straight to Hell before he'd come after her again, like a puppy.

Jennifer ran for what seemed a very long time, the night air tearing in her throat. She felt as if her eyes were shedding fire rather than tears. She hurt all over, but she wasn't sure why. It all seemed so confused, so very terribly jumbled. He'd deserved her blows! *Deserved* them, the unfeeling little snot! He was just like all the other men, brutish, inconsiderate. Honor? Philosophy? Ploys that confused not only women, but men themselves. As if women weren't breathing, thinking humans, too!

Oliver was condescending, just like all the rest. Most of

them had their heads in the clouds and their feet sunk in filthy quicksand.

A cold moon peeked through nodding tree branches. The smells of growing things and humus rode the whispering breeze.

Jennifer barely noticed them. Her mind was afire. Despite her closeness to Oliver, despite their shared thoughts and emotions, they were yet strangers. The horror was that this was the way *he* seemed to *want* it!

Somewhere nearby an owl hooted.

She looked up. Where was she? Some starlit glade, a good cry's distance from the van. Which way had she come?

That way, she figured. She began to walk. A shiver of fear touched her. She moved faster. Why hadn't Oliver run after her? Of course. His pride. Well, she'd have to live with that. A strange thing, pride. People confused it with dignity, which is being what you truly are. Pride, though, is being what you *think* you are.

Suddenly, a voice called from the darkness. "Jennifer!"

She jumped. "Oliver! Is that you?"

Darkness lay thick before her and she could not make out any form. The moons had ducked behind clouds.

"Jennifer! Jennifer, dearest, come here!"

She would have run, but the voice was familiar.

In the darkness a face suddenly appeared, framed in light. Neat hair. Beard. Friendly, caring eyes. It smiled at her kindly.

"Father!" Pure, unreasoning excitement filled Jennifer as she recognized the face. "Father!"

She ran toward him.

The waiting jabberwock raised its claws.

Frantically, Oliver paced.

"Why did you let her go?" Penton asked sleepily, mist from steaming tea rising into his face. It was his watch.

"I don't know. Why did she go?"

"Sir, when women get like that, you don't know *what* they'll do! Most likely something self-destructive. I shouldn't worry about it, though. She'll be back."

"If anything happens to her, it's all my fault!"

Penton stepped by the fire, warming his feet. "No, it's not. I dare say you won't be getting any sleep, so you can just sit here with me. We'll talk."

Oliver ran his fingers through his hair. "Penton. What

would I do without you? I don't know *why* you tag along with me. I truly don't."

Penton closed his eyes and did not respond. Closed up within himself, the manservant seemed to be huddling protectively over some private thought.

Oliver was too preoccupied to dwell much on what was going on inside Caspar Penton's head. "I'm going to get MacPherson up. We have to look for her," Oliver said.

"As you say, sir."

Oliver strode to the van. Deep snores sounded from its interior. MacPherson wouldn't like this much, but—

From the woods, a figure stepped into the flickering shadows caused by the firelight.

Stopping short, surprised, Oliver said, "Jennifer!" He could not restrain the relief he felt at seeing her. He went to her. "Jennifer, are you all right? Where have you been? I've been so worried." He turned toward Penton. "Penton! She's back! She's fine!"

"What did you say, sir?" Penton said. Then he saw that Jennifer had returned. "Ah. Quite. You two should get some sleep now."

Turning back to Jennifer, Oliver said, "Listen. Jenny, I'm sorry I said all those things. Please, forgive me. Will you?"

She smiled at him. "Of course. But we must talk, Oliver. We *must* have a long talk."

"Yes. Yes, of course, dear. We'll have the talk in the morning. You must be cold. Can I get you a blanket?"

"*Now*, Oliver. It's very important. We must talk now. Privately."

"If you insist. I suppose we should get this business buried, right?" *Dammit*, he thought. *Dolan, you're being a puppy dog again, eager to please.* But he couldn't help his joy at seeing her alive and well and evidently willing to forgive. She did look a bit mussed. Her hair was a delightful mess of curls and bits of forest. Her clothes were rumpled. But she was here and alive, and if she wanted to talk, he would talk. Surely it wouldn't be long.

Casually, a relaxed smile showing in the lace of shadows and light from the fire, she reached out, took his hand softly in hers. A momentarily cold hand, it soon warmed with the touch of his palm and his intertwining fingers.

An inward peace flowed through Oliver as she turned and began to lead him away. It was all right. Everything was all right. He could feel already the delightful rhythms of her being, the light of her mind, that their closeness had created these long, strange weeks. *One,* she had said before. *We are one, Oliver. We know each other, need each other, are each other. It's love, Oliver, and more than love. We will never, never leave each other. We are inseparable.*

Now he thought, *Yes. Yes, perhaps my struggle is perverse. I do know her.*

She stopped for a moment, turned her head a bit. Shadow obscured all but a sliver of her dusky face. "In my walk, I discovered a place where the grass is growing already. We shall sit there, Oliver, and talk."

Emotion choked his throat. He could not speak. He let a nod suffice.

She led him on until he could no longer see the firelight of their camp.

The soft silent mouth of the night swallowed them with its insistent darkness.

MacPherson stumbled to his knees.

He held his hands together and began to pray for guidance.

He closed his eyes to the wealth of spring around him, to the smells and the tastes of the glen. He did not hear the birds, or the stirrings of the tree limbs as the wind soughed through them. He directed all his being into his prayer.

Sometimes the Lord God replied, but He never actually responded to MacPherson's requests; that bothered MacPherson. Nonetheless, when the Voice came, its mere sound in his mind was almost enough. It reassured the man of his Creator's existence.

"Dear Heavenly Father," he prayed. "I need Your aid more than ever this day. For I have sinned in my heart with the woman, Jennifer Eden. She has given me seductive looks, and my heart burns with her glance, my loins respond to her smile. Protect me from this sin, God. I entreat You, to answer me this time. I have done as You asked; I go on this journey. Now I but ask You tell me how to deal with these dreadful feelings, that I might complete my task, and that I might save my wretched soul from Your wrath that will surely follow, should I succumb."

MacPherson waited, head bowed.

No answer came.

MacPherson fell onto his face in the dead leaves, in great despair. She was so very beautiful, so very alluring, and he wanted to touch her more than anything he had ever—

"My goodness, dear man!" a voice said from behind him. "Are you well?"

Roald MacPherson rolled over. Standing above him was Jennifer Eden, her hair wild, her eyes the most beautiful things that the man had ever seen in all his days.

"Here, let me help you up," she said. Her hands brushed his hair as they slipped down to his shoulders. She kneeled by him. "You poor dear fellow. You need love too, don't you? Well, we have time. They've camped for the night, and they won't suspect."

"No," he said as her hair caressed his cheek.

He made no further objection.

III: 6

As THE VAN covered the short distance remaining to Computer Mountain, Oliver swam in a daze of blood.

He handled his duties with the usual competence, maintaining a veneer of sociability with Penton and MacPherson. Somehow, though, his body seemed not to be his, nor his words, nor even his thoughts. He was just a bag of blood on legs. His only joy lay in the darkness and Jennifer's mouth.

"Wake up," she said, patting him on his back as he lay curled in his sleeping bag beside the ashes of the campfire. "I'm hungry."

"Yes," he said. He groped for his shoes, put them on. Dawn was spurting red on the horizon. All was quiet; not even MacPherson's snores broke the stillness of the morning.

"Soon we will truly be together, Oliver. Just a day or so —then our true lives will start."

"Yes," Oliver said.

"It's a bit cold this morning, dear heart. I've brought your heavy coat from the van. We'll go only a short distance. After we enter the Mountain, we will not have to hide our love any longer."

Yes. The Mountain. They had to visit the Mountain, which was quite close. Oliver did not recognize it, nor did he care much. The Einstein had confirmed that Computer Mountain lay just ahead, though only in the last hour of the previous day had it slowly reared above them. Just a *small* mountain, insignificant, green like all the other slowly rolling mountains around them.

Oliver didn't care much.

The morning was cold. Oliver was already numb, so he barely felt the chill. Still, he put on the coat that Jennifer gave him, and Jennifer took him by the arm.

They walked a ways, through the sudden spring.

"You have been very good, Oliver. They cannot know of our full bond yet."

"I—I do my best, for you."

"Tell me again, Oliver, what you said last night." Her voice was sweet and gay.

"I cannot live . . . without you."

"We will sleep together always, side by side," she said. "We will have more children than I *ever* dreamed." She smiled, showing lovely white teeth. "They will all be like me. You will be like me. The way it is *supposed* to be."

"The way it is supposed to be."

"How do you feel about me?" They brushed past some ferns into a small glade ringed by bushes dotted with small red berries. "How beautiful am I, Oliver?"

"You are the most beautiful woman I have ever seen."

"You used to recite poetry sometimes."

" 'In Xanadu did Kubla Khan, a stately pleasure dome decree'—"

Jennifer interrupted. "No. You made it up. About *me!*"

"I cannot. Not now."

"You're not thinking about some other woman?"

"No. No, I'm not thinking at all."

"I will never forgive that hussy who thought she could take you away from me. She has already joined our number. But you will not see her again, will you?"

"No, never."

She stopped him. "This is a wonderful place," she said, gesturing to soft green new grass poking through a layer of brown leaves. "Lie down, Oliver."

Oliver lay down. Jennifer kneeled down beside him.

"Take off the scarf."

Oliver obeyed.

Jennifer smiled, satisfied. "You are very near completion, Oliver. Soon the soft darkness will be yours as well as mine. We will be joined. We will be one. We will join a community of brothers and sisters and lovers. But I will not take much this morning, for you must not join us yet. You must obey my orders, see this mission of yours to completion for the sake of our beloved Master. Do you understand?"

"Yes."

"I thought you would."

Looking up through the red haze that surrounded him, he could see her bending over him, hair falling like a shroud. She smelled of unnatural perfume, a choking, cloying scent. Her mouth touched his throat, softly and delicately, recalling her touch after her return to the encampment.

She bit into him. There was no pain now. Rather, the pain was welcomed, somehow transformed into pleasure.

155

The rhythmic sucking sounds were the music of their combining. His mind seemed to reach out, touch hers, mesh once more, moving in paths of her direction.

"We will serve him, Oliver."

He felt the blood flow from him. The sensation was almost ecstatic, a release of pressure, tension. The dull lethargy was delicious, the perfect ease. If he had had the strength, he would have wrapped his arms around her. But he was content just to lie there while she absorbed his blood and soul.

Dimly he could make out a dissonance. A man, crying out: "Witch! Demon of the Devil!"

He opened his eyes.

Jennifer kneeled above him, eyes afire. Her open mouth revealed scalpel-sharp fangs. Blood smeared her chin, and the interior of her mouth was bright with it. She hissed.

Oliver recognized someone. It was Roald MacPherson, who stood a few yards distant, holding his rapier, swaying dizzily. The collar of his shirt was open, the first buttons undone. Two livid marks rode low on his neck.

He advanced, wobbling.

"Stop!" Jennifer commanded.

MacPherson halted. "I must kill you. To save my soul, I must—"

She stood, smiling confidently. "You must only drop your weapon."

"No. No, I must—"

"I tell you what is to be, don't you remember? Didn't I make that clear last night?"

He tried to avoid her gaze, but failed. Their eyes locked. The sword dropped, switching off.

"Very good, MacPherson," she said, voice sweet again. "Now, you will never, *ever* do that again, will you? You men are a stubborn lot."

"Yes, we are, Jennifer."

Caspar Penton stood at the clearing's edge, holding a gun.

"So you know," Jennifer said, still smiling.

"Yes, Jennifer. Now I do. Or should I call you Paler? Jennifer is gone, isn't she? You've got her."

"That gun will do you no good," Jennifer said, standing. "We are more than human. Why don't you give up? My friends here have. It's not so bad, Penton. In fact, it's quite pleasurable. I rather fancy you, Penton. Always have. You're the virile sort, you know? I like that. We can get to know one another."

"You've no subtlety, Paler. Bit too brazen to be tempting."

"Don't anger me, I warn you."

"Ah, ha! A sense of humor about everything save your almighty ego. Well, you know, actually I'd be sensitive about that too, Paler. You're not so much. Using an innocent girl!"

"Innocent? If she were so innocent, I could not have used her. I have her memories here, Mr. Penton. I blush. *My* genius for manipulation is rebuked."

"Ah, but all of that is simply the way she was trained, Paler. The traps of society. The stupidities and perfidies of this particular human culture. She was a good person, Paler. She did nothing bad; she was, at times, delightful. I shall miss her. You, however, are worthless scum. I suggest you cease and desist your petty game and let us be about our business. Then we will parley."

"Never! You presume too much."

"Ah. Then I suppose I'll just have to go back and get one of those explosive stakes. A shame I didn't bring one with me, but then I didn't know what was truly afoot until now."

"You will not!" Jennifer shouted.

"How are you going to stop me? With the body of a frail girl? You've used her charms and wiles and beauty quite well, dear chap—seems to have come natural to you. But I'm afraid that you're dealing with a man of experience— not a lovesick young man or a frustrated celibate. Now, if you'll excuse me, I'll go back and get something."

MacPherson struggled to stand, fell back. "The sword, man!"

"Oh my, yes. I should have known you'd bring that, MacPherson. Ah ha! There it is. That should do the trick." Penton walked forward to where the sword lay in a bed of leaves.

"No!" With a flurry of hair and skirts, Jennifer hurled herself toward the sword as well.

Penton fired his revolver.

The first bullet took her full in the chest, and she staggered. The second hurled her to the ground. She fell, and almost immediately stood again.

Penton grimaced with distaste. He advanced and fired again. And again. The bullets did not kill the vampire, but their impact prevented her reaching the sword.

As Penton reached down to scoop the hilt up, Jennifer cried, "MacPherson! Stop him!"

Obviously filled with turmoil, MacPherson leaped for Penton, dragging him to the ground, knocking the gun away.

"Hold him there," Paler commanded through Jennifer's bloody form.

Whimpering, MacPherson obeyed.

Jennifer smiled and stood. Her chest smoked from the bullet holes in her blouse. Confidently, she strode toward Penton, who wriggled in MacPherson's strong embrace. "Good God, man! Let me go!"

Jennifer kneeled by Penton.

"Oliver!"

"Oh, he's long gone, dear chap."

Dainty hands reached out.

Only dimly aware of what transpired, Oliver Dolan watched. He lay on one side, numb.

"Oliver!" Penton cried desperately. "You gutless little twit! Spineless mother's boy! Harpy-ridden fool! She's finally got you where she wants you!"

Somewhere deep inside of Oliver, a tiny spark was fanned to burning life by Penton's words.

"You're just a pawn, and always *have* been. You've been so used, you're finally used up, hey?"

The flame grew. Memories tumbled over end into growing heat, igniting themselves. His mother. Anziel. Jennifer. Paler.

He stood and walked to where the sword lay. He picked it up by the hilt. His thumb found the control tab. He pressed it. In the still glade the electric crackle of the laser sword was easily heard.

Jennifer lifted her mouth from Penton's neck and turned.

Expressionless, Oliver swung the rapier with all his strength.

The headless body fell, thrashed a moment, then was still. Blood was splashed over everything.

MacPherson mumbled, "I am freed."

Penton, holding his wounded neck, got to his feet. "You can turn the sword off now, sir."

Oliver nodded. The sword blinked off.

Penton put his hand to the young man's shoulder. "Thank you. I only said those things to free you of your daze, you know. It was our only hope."

Oliver closed his eyes and began to walk away. "We have a journey to complete," he said in a hard whisper.

Penton said, "We should bury her first, don't you think?"

Stopping in his tracks, Oliver turned slowly. He looked down at the corpse and the blood. His hands began to tremble.

"Let her rot."

Hands to neck, Vlad Paler cried out.

He tried to rise, but stumbled and fell hard onto the floor, trailing the wires that connected his headband to a large machine. He gasped and sputtered. His attendants hurried to his side.

"Lord Paler!"

"Get it off my head!"

Fingers pried the band and wires from his skull. Breathing heavily, Paler managed to gasp, "Get me a brandy!"

He was helped back into the chair. A glass of brandy was pressed into his hand. He drained it in a gulp.

Dammit, how had that happened? He had them, had them all, there in that clearing. How had Dolan wrenched from his control? He had *felt* that blade slicing through the neck of Jennifer Eden. It had all happened too quickly to disengage contact and control. He had *died* there in that clearing.

Shaking uncontrollably despite the soothing of the brandy, he leaped to his feet. "Prepare the jabberwock contact!" he cried. "I want complete control of the thing!"

He strode toward the equipment that would link him with Darkwing. Anger overcoming reason, Paler stormed into the interlock chamber. If he could surprise them before they reached their van . . .

Then jaws would bite and claws would catch!

"It wasn't her fault, you know," Penton said.

Oliver did not answer.

"MacPherson is burying her. Saying a few words. Do you want to pay your last respects?" He sighed. "Paler must have gotten her that time she ran off. After your argument."

Oliver lay on the ground where he'd fallen. He could barely move. One moment he'd been striding determinedly for the van, the next he was gasping upon the ground.

She was dead. He had killed her.

"*Someone* would have had to kill her, sir."

"Yes." He stared down at the ground.

"We of the living must press on, sir."

"I don't know if I want to live anymore."

"Well, sir. If you die in your condition, Paler would have you. Do you want that?"

"No!" Oliver snapped.

"Well then, you must stay alive a little longer."

"I'm trapped."

"Yes. Aren't we all."

MacPherson rejoined them. "Dug a hole for her in the loam," he said. "Threw some dirt over her. She will rest peacefully now. Her soul—her soul is where it belongs now."

MacPherson leaned over and placed his hand under Oliver's arm, half in comfort, half in preparation to help him up. "You did what I could not do, Oliver Dolan. You did what I did not have the strength or courage to do."

Oliver looked up at Penton. "Maybe I did it for the wrong reason."

He brushed the assisting hand away brusquely. Curtly, he stood, attempting to straighten his hopelessly disheveled clothes. He was spattered with blood. "Maybe it was the real Jennifer I struck at."

"She was *gone,*" MacPherson said. "You know that—"

Penton said, "Yes, and in this case, the end justifies the means."

Oliver shot him an angry look. Then he struck ahead into the forest.

They reached the clearing where the van had been parked.

"Oh, God!" Penton said. He groped for his pistol.

MacPherson drew his sword.

Oliver Dolan stared wearily at the thing, not wanting to believe his eyes. Though he'd seen jabberwocks before, they were certainly not common. He'd never known one to attack, for they were generally cowardly beasts, ferocious on the surface, but backing off when it came to a fight.

When this jabberwock raised itself from its perch on the van, Oliver could see it was no normal jabberwock. A flickering screen stuck from its chest. After a moment, a man's face showed on it. The face reflected hatred and resolve.

The jabberwock flapped its wobbly wings, lifted from the van's roof toward them, claws outstretched, fanged mouth open and drooling.

"Split up!" Oliver commanded. "Somebody's got to get inside the van!"

MacPherson dodged to the left, Penton to the right.

Oliver, weaponless, chose to retreat to the comparative safety of a nearby copse of elm trees.

With a horrifying yell, the jabberwock advanced. Caspar Penton aimed his revolver, fired. From the beast's abdomen blood dripped.

The jabberwock veered toward its immediate attacker.

Penton, crouching, fired again. The bullet tore off one of the beast's membranous ears.

Backing off immediately, Penton dug into his pocket for more ammunition. While he cracked open the weapon to insert two shells, the jabberwock attacked with a burst of speed, flinging a claw madly at the temporarily defenseless man. Penton ducked and rolled. A claw just missed him. He snapped the gun closed, aimed. The claw returned, slapping him backhanded two yards into some mulberry bushes. The pistol fell to the ground. Penton lay unconscious, bleeding from the mouth.

The jabberwock pressed in, claws unsheathed. A smirk showed from the screen.

Oliver darted madly from the trees. His only hope was the pistol. If MacPherson could reach the van . . . He ran, but blood loss had weakened him considerably.

MacPherson headed not for the van, but to save Penton. His sword hissed into the beast's side, biting through metal and flesh. Dark smoke rose from the beast.

With a mad cry of pain, the jabberwock twisted around.

A crack sounded. The light of the sword winked out. The sword had been broken. Astonished, MacPherson fell back, holding only the hilt. He tried a crab crawl backward. Almost immediately the jabberwock was upon him. MacPherson's cry died quickly.

Oliver did not stop to watch. He raced for the fallen pistol, dived, and came up holding the thing wrong way around. The beast swerved to face him. Oliver fumbled a moment, then squeezed the trigger. The hammer clicked onto an empty chamber.

The jabberwock shambled toward him. Blood dripped from its side. Shorn wires dangled. Otherwise it seemed unimpaired.

Save for the beast's head.

The face no longer glared. Its expression showed great pain. The head drooped. The body, however, was clearly fired by some fiercer power. And that face . . . that face in the tube. Oliver realized that it must be Vlad Paler.

"You *bastard!*" Oliver screamed, raising his weapon.

The man laughed delightedly. "I shall not harm your body too much, dear fellow. I *need* it."

Then the jabberwock's head straightened, seeming to recover. Terror crossed its face. The jaw worked briefly, then the creature spoke: "Cor blimey, not me 'ead! I can't 'elp myself! Shoot the tube! Shoot the picture tube!"

Oliver paused.

Taking a chance, he lowered his aim from the beast's head to Vlad Paler's grim face. He fired. The bullet struck the screen dead center.

The jabberwock slowed, pain showing clearly on its face. "Not enough!" he cried. "Again!"

Oliver aimed, put another bullet into the mechanism.

"Damn!" Paler's voice cried. "You can't—" Then the voice sputtered out in a crackle of static.

The jabberwock stopped in its tracks. It stared down at its smoking chest. "Oh God! I'm on fire!"

"Who are you?" Oliver demanded.

"Help me get this fire out, or I'm a goner!" The jabberwock flailed at its massive chest with its paws. The air smelled of burned insulation and charred flesh.

Oliver paused, then made his decision. He ran to the van, pulled open the door, and grabbed the extinguisher labeled ELECTRICAL, then scrambled back to where the jabberwock lay on its side, howling and weeping.

Oliver advanced cautiously. When close enough, he stuck the nozzle into the beast's chest and sprayed.

"I'm dying!" the jabberwock cried. Huge tears dripped forlornly from limpid eyes. "I'm a goner!"

Carefully, Oliver backed away from the claws. "Well, fire's out. I think you'll survive."

"The bloody bomb!" The jabberwock's eyes widened.

"Pardon!"

"He stuck a bomb inside me, too! Get away! Far away, Oliver Dolan. Take your manservant. He's going to detonate me any moment."

"I'll be damned if he will," Oliver said. He raced to the van, and quickly returned with clippers and screwdrivers. "Where's the bomb!"

"I deserve to die!" the jabberwock sniveled.

"Oh. In that case—"

"No! Wait!" the jabberwock said. "Behind and above the screen circuitry."

Oliver strode forward determinedly. He took a glove

from his pocket, put it on, and picked at glass and snarled wires.

The beast's chest heaved. A wisp of smoke emerged from the cavity.

"Steady on, fellow. You'll have to keep still, or I won't be able to work."

The jabberwock managed to quiet its breathing.

"Ah. Yes. I see it," Oliver said. "Simple enough. I'll just cut one of the leads."

The jabberwock put its paws to its ears, closed its eyes, and whimpered.

Oliver snipped twice.

He took a breath. He was still alive.

"I beat him!" he said jubilantly.

The jabberwock opened his eyes. "You *did* it! I'm forever grateful!" His head lay limp, his tongue lolled. "I'm going to kill the bleeder, I swear it! I didn't want to do any of it. *Any* of it. I'm sorry. I'm going to change my ways. I swear to God, I'm going to be a new jabberwock. If I live."

"You sound healthy enough to me. A little burned, a little nicked. Evidently, MacPherson's blade cut the control override cables to your head, and you were able to speak."

"You're bloody right! That poor chap! I killed him, didn't I?"

Oliver glanced to where MacPherson's ragged body lay, then averted his gaze. "I'd say so, yes. But it wasn't you. It was Paler."

"He—he made me kill the girl. I . . . felt . . . so awful," the jabberwock gasped. "I hate myself."

"Yes, well, join the club."

"You *believe* me. You'd believe a jabberwock?" The eyes opened wide, a little astonished.

"If I didn't, you'd be dead now."

"Yes. Yes, I would. And I wouldn't blame you for a moment."

"Stay there," Oliver said, suddenly remembering Penton. He hurried to the man who lay draped over a bush.

As Oliver pulled him to his feet, Penton roused. "Shall I draw a bath for you, sir?" he said, blearily looking at Oliver. "You seem to have had a dirty day."

"No. No, Penton. That won't be necessary."

"In that case, I believe I will resume my nap."

He collapsed into Oliver's arms.

III: 7

SOMEHOW THE MOUNTAIN seemed smaller than before. Still, there could be no doubt that it was *the* Mountain.

The familiar gates remained, dulled now, and all around lay piles of jumbled, rusting mechanisms, nightcreatures destroyed by the laser fire of Anziel Dubrelizy's starship.

Oliver halted the van and engaged the safety brake, then patted Penton softly on the shoulder. "Well, my friend, this is Computer Mountain."

"Good Lord, sir!" Penton's gaze moved from pile to rust-red pile. He was silent a moment. Then he noticed the movement of a shadow. He started, but relaxed almost at once. "I believe our moaning friend is wondering what we're going to do next."

"Hmm?" Oliver looked up from his work over an equipment pile, mostly weapons.

Darkwing was peering mournfully through the windshield. His chest was black from the fire of the day before and his side bore a long seam from the laser sword. Penton had replaced the jabberwock's ear, then cleaned and closed the other bullet wound while the jabberwock retold the story of Hampton's loss and the subsequent degradations to which Paler had put him. Penton and Oliver learned a great deal about the Vampire Lord and his plans in the process. They had agreed that the jabberwock could accompany them to Computer Mountain, in return for his aid.

Darkwing was not so sure about aid, but he went along, he claimed, as much for the company as anything.

"Doesn't look as if he cares much for the look of all those dead nightcreatures, does he?" Oliver said.

"You should explain where they came from," Penton suggested. "He might not want to enter with us. Though he *could* be useful."

Oliver readied the weapons, then stepped out the rear to speak with the creature. "How would you like to visit your birthplace, Darkwing?"

Darkwing was not enthusiastic.

*   *   *

The van's headlights thrust aside the darkness of the tunnel as it moved slowly forward. Hesitantly, Darkwing crept along behind.

The passageway was as Oliver remembered it, save that no lights, guide or otherwise, were lit. He'd always planned to return, but he'd never had the opportunity. They had to stop at the elevators because the wider passageways had been blocked.

"You guard the van," Oliver said to Darkwing as he and Penton dismounted.

"Not bloody likely I'll go exploring."

Gripping pistols, Oliver and Penton approached the closest elevator. Oliver hit the OPEN button.

The door obediently parted.

"*Déjà vu,*" Oliver sighed. He entered and Penton followed. Oliver pushed the button marked DOWN.

The moving box deposited them in the large chamber where, before, demons had capered and Satan's giant robot had stalked them. Now, no pseudohellfire glowed, no voices sounded. Oliver picked their way with a flashlight.

Minutes later, they found the passageway that led to where Satan had lain in his nutrient bath, his being meshed with the great computer system.

The flashlight began to quiver.

"Still a bit weak, sir?" Penton asked.

"No. This place still scares the hell out of me."

"I don't blame you."

They entered a great hall and descended the ramp into a corridor. A smell accosted them. Mummified flesh. "That will be the remains of Nicholas, his demons, and maybe a few other nightcreatures," Oliver said, his voice muffled.

"And Turner?"

"Yes." Oliver's voice was strained. "And Turner."

"If this is too much for you, sir, I can advance on my own."

"No, I'll be all right, Penton. Thank you. I've faced many unpleasant things recently. I suppose I can face one more." He sighed. "Besides, perhaps we should bury the old fellow."

The hallway opened into Satan's personal chamber. The cone of the flashlight spread into the darkness, revealing numerous dessicated demon corpses.

"Evidently plenty of bacteria hereabouts," Penton commented.

The light moved on to the tank, which held only a mass

of greenish sludge by this time. A skull lay at one end, an eyesocket visible through the slime.

"Meet Satan, Penton."

Penton tipped his hat. "Pleased to make your acquaintance."

"If we only knew where the main control complex was." Oliver raised his voice. "Computer! Are you listening? What is happening here? We need to talk to you!"

The lights came on immediately. "Welcome." The voice was a monotone. "You are expected."

Oliver and Penton jumped.

The voice continued: "At the far side of the room is a lever. Push, and a shaft will be exposed. Climb the shaft. What you seek awaits you there."

"Ask and ye shall receive," Penton said. "Let's be off."

"Wait," Oliver whispered.

"What's wrong, sir? We've got what we want."

Oliver was gazing down at the floor. He pointed. "I left him here." He looked up, astonished. "I left Geoffrey Turner here, dead, I swear to God!"

The floor was bare.

The large room was brightly lit by electroluminescents; computer consoles, switchboards, and telemetry equipment were everywhere. None seemed to be operating.

In a large console chair sat Geoffrey Turner—what remained of him.

Oliver was so astonished that he dropped the handkerchief from his mouth though the odor of decayed flesh was almost overwhelming. He walked slowly forward.

The corpse in the chair had lost most of its flesh. Its tattered suit was just a mass of loose folds. The dead skin was drawn tight over its skull; eyes and nose were long gone.

"I swear, he was dead as a door knocker!"

"Yes, well, he's certainly dead enough now. Looks as if he had enough life to crawl up here. Maybe he reprogrammed the computer or something. Looks as if that was what he was attempting. He's got wires wrapped all around him . . . even connected through his back! See?"

Oliver had recovered sufficiently to notice that—yes, wires did trail off. Penton must have it right. Somehow Turner had revived long enough to truly expire here. But dammit, he had died. He said he was dying, and he did die. Oliver turned away from Geoffrey Turner's body, sick at heart.

Penton examined the console closely. "Now, there must be a button here which activates the computer fully. Do you know anything about these things, sir?"

Sighing, somehow no longer terribly interested, Oliver directed his attention to the board. Perhaps he could have done something for Turner. "No," he said. "No, I suppose we'll just have to get it by trial and error."

From behind him, a hand fell lightly to Oliver's shoulder. A mechanical croak: "Th-that . . . r-rred . . . one."

Peripherally, Oliver noticed a bony hand, raised and pointing.

He spun around. The dead body of Geoffrey Turner wobbled beside the chair for a moment, then tumbled into its former place. The left hand struck the plastic of the chair's arm and several fingers clattered to the metal floor.

Oliver Dolan fainted dead away.

"Here, drink this."

"No. No more blood. No more blood."

"Tastier than blood, Oliver, I assure you." Cool metal brushed his lips, then liquid was flowing into his mouth.

Stinging brandy trickled warmly down his throat. Suddenly he realized where he was. He turned his head to find that Penton was supporting him with one hand, the flask was in the other.

In the momentary silence, a harsh voice enunciated slowly: "I . . . would . . . that . . . I . . . could . . . have . . . a . . . drop."

The voice emerged from a nearby speaker grille.

"Geoffrey!"

The body remained stationary.

"Not much of him left, I'm afraid," Penton said. "We're here just in time. Failing fast."

"It . . . is . . . good . . . to . . . have . . . you . . . here."

"You may save that for later, Mr. Turner. I'll play the tape you've prepared to explain things. Then we'll see what we can do."

The voice did not respond.

Oliver was still aghast. "But he's dead! How can he talk to us!"

"Yes, he's dead. At least his fleshly part, obviously. But as you yourself discovered, sir, Mr. Turner was a mandroid or, rather, to be technically correct, a cyborg—part flesh, part robot. Evidently something of his personality lingered in the circuits of his robot self. It was Turner who called us here somehow. What a tremendous feat of willpower, surviving, let alone occasionally controlling the computer. He's plugged himself into it! While you were—um, indisposed, he told me that, expecting us, he has recorded a message that will explain the next step." Penton placed the flask firmly in Oliver's hand, then walked to the control board, immediately flicking a switch.

A much smoother voice issued from the speaker.

"It is difficult," the voice said. "I am . . . quite . . . not quite in control. If you are listening to these words—" Suddenly an incomprehensible electronic babble began to emerge from the speaker. Distant voices screeched. Something like thunder bellowed in the background. "You must attach," the voice continued, lucidly. "You must attach the Einstein you have brought. It will know what to do."

The voice died away into a chorus of shouts and cries.

Suddenly a voice shouted, "The Lord God has spoken!"

Eyes wide, Penton switched off the tape. "Well, that's about it. You better now, sir?"

Oliver managed to struggle to his feet, averting his eyes from Turner's corpse. "Yes, I think so."

"Then we'd better fetch the Einstein, hadn't we? That's what he wants."

After some fairly strenuous exertions, Penton and Oliver managed to move the box down through the tunnels to Turner's apparent final resting place.

"Don't strain yourself too much—Mr. Turner? But you must tell us how to connect the Einstein and yourself."

"There is a plug. Place . . . in . . . jack . . . X . . . oh . . . one."

"I believe he means this one, sir," Penton said, unreeling a lead from the Electrical Mind Clone. He connected it to the indicated hole.

Suddenly screeches erupted. Tumultuous yells and screams, as if a battle were taking place inside the computer. Geoffrey Turner's corpse spasmed and patches of dry skin flaked from its head, emphasizing the skull's death leer.

Then, as suddenly as they had begun, the sounds died away and the room filled with a haze of bluish-gray smoke, dimming those lights still on. The Electrical Mind Clone was dark as well.

"What was *that?*" Oliver asked numbly.

"Goodness knows," Penton replied, coughing. He rose

from his crouch, brushing off his coat. "Sounded like all Hell breaking loose."

The Einstein's lights flickered to life. "As a matter of fact, it's something very much like that, Mr. Penton."

"Geoffrey!" Oliver said, crawling over to the machine, scrutinizing it. "Is that really you. I mean, *really* you? I mean, I did see you die, didn't I?"

"Questions, questions. Well, to begin with, I happen to know, Oliver Dolan, that you had a bed-wetting problem until the age of eight."

Oliver blushed. "I did tell you that, didn't I?"

"You told me a great deal, dear chap. Much of which I've forgotten. That part of me which is the Mind Clone barely knows you at all. So we'll have to get reacquainted, won't we?"

"How did you survive?" Penton asked.

"Actually, I didn't. I died, truly I did. A glorious and meaningful death too—wasn't it, Oliver?"

"I confess," Penton said. "I was moved by its retelling."

"Oh, excellent. Well, yes, my fat old body ceased functioning, beaten by that wretched robot and those awful demons. I thought for sure that I was boarding the ferry. Otherwise, I might have asked Oliver to linger on. Alas, I confess, with the mission complete, I was ready to call it a day. Five centuries is a wearisome bit of time."

"But you didn't die!" Oliver said.

"I *did* die, Oliver. You felt my pulse, didn't you? You can see that dreadful husk in that chair over there, can't you? That was a real charmer to be stuck in for all that time. No. You see, for all my knowledge of my construction, I assumed that once the biological aspects of the mandroidal body ceased, it naturally followed that the mechanical aspects would as well. But I'd failed to take into account the self-recharging battery that powered the limb extensors and life-support equipment. Obviously more of me was microchips and machinery than I ever wanted to admit. So, my body died and commenced to—um, decompose.

"But the next thing I knew, I was alive again. Perhaps I should say I *returned*. However, my eyes by then being gone, to say nothing of most other senses, I was rather in the dark, don't you know."

"How did you reach *here,* then?"

"Well you might wonder, Penton. I knew where I was. I knew the layout of the chambers, and I retained a kind of rough sense of touch. I could detect vibrations. Most important, though, I could sense and follow electricity flows—it's part of the life-support circuitry. Thus, once my batteries were fully charged, I managed to crawl to the nearest wall. A few weeks later I managed to figure where the exit I needed was, and how to open it. By my calculations, it took me several months to finally make my way up here, having to stop often to recharge the old battery. Naturally, my destination was this computer room where I hoped to connect myself to the computer. Alas, Nicholas's own connections were no longer functional, else I would have used *them*. Fortunately, I learned a great deal of patience in my centuries, or I fear I would have languished with depression. I might very well have, though, if I knew what was waiting for me."

"Which was?" Oliver asked, entranced.

"As you can see, I managed to connect myself. What a terrific chore *that* was. Each movement was a terrific difficulty. Well, once the interface was completed, what was waiting for me almost did me in! You see, at that time, the computer was principally dormant. The problem was that dear old Nicholas had put so much of himself into the computer, the computer itself had become psychotic."

"I don't understand," Penton said.

"Wait a moment," Oliver interrupted. "Are you saying, Geoffrey, that the inside of this computer was the terrain of Hedley Nicholas's madness? His perception of Hell and his Kingdom. Demons . . ."

"More than that, he had his own paper heaven celestially aloft. Angels . . . Gracious me, it really was stunning. What a warped imagination the man had. Better than Milton's! When I intruded, in my somewhat shaky shape—you see, I was a little crackers myself—the computer immediately concluded God Himself was intruding. Well, as you can imagine, there was conflict. To protect my sense of self, I immediately assumed the personality the computer expected, thus gaining the power it deemed proper to God. Self-fulfilling prophecy, for sure, that. But I had something. At times, in my less lucid moments, I actually believed I *was* God. Can you imagine that?" Laughter issued from the Einstein. "Me, the atheist! Well, in that fray is a whole story in itself. Suffice it to say, I had little time to allot to the outside world. Alas, Satan's connections to his night-creatures he maintained entirely within his own mind and they were freed. I could not recontact. When I could, I

170

performed signal scans, tried to encode autonomy-mode overrides and, occasionally, selective security destructs—with some unusual responses, particularly lately, that I have not yet been able to interpret. In the event, none seem to have worked as the manuals describe. Some time back, though, in Satan's waking chambers I came across one of his experiments and managed to alter it sufficiently to serve my needs."

"MacPherson!" Oliver cried. "That explains MacPherson! And you made the sword for him!"

"Spot of work, that, but I managed. Sent him out to learn what was going on. Also to find HOPE and the Einstein. Mostly, though, to find you, Oliver. I knew I could trust you to return."

"Why didn't MacPherson *tell* us all this?" Penton asked. "He could have made the whole thing quite clear."

"Yes. Well, I *did* mention that I—well, dammit, I wasn't functioning properly. I was pretty well gone, and the computer damn near had a will of its own!"

"Go ahead, Geoffrey," Oliver said. "You don't have to be ashamed. You were almost an extension of the computer, because you needed to act out Satan's conception of God."

A long silence ensued, followed by a simple, "Close. Very close. I can't begin to communicate to you the actual situation."

"Yes. Yes, you are quite right."

"So, once we brought the Einstein here and connected it to you," Penton continued, "you had sufficient power and personality to defeat that portion of the computer that still had the concepts with which you warred."

"Well, I drove them away for a while, anyway. Hard to say when they'll resurface. Right now, the computer is just a normal computer. I do believe we can go on with something constructive."

"Which is?"

"Very simple, if a trifle time-consuming. First, utilizing the laboratory facilities now at our disposal, we must discover the cure for the wretched disease this fellow Paler has concocted, mustn't we?"

"You know of Paler, then?" Penton asked.

"I know all that MacPherson knew. I know all that my Mind Clone knew, for I am presently bonded with it."

"*Then* we will deal with Paler."

"Yes. But in the meantime, there is something else I

171

want to do. You see, besides the complete memory the Einstein holds, it also carried something else rather close to my heart, so to speak."

"Which is?" Oliver asked.

"Quite simply, the genetic code of my biological self. With the incredible technology at my disposal here, it will be easy enough, with your help, to build another Geoffrey Turner."

"Geoffrey!" Oliver said. "You'll be able to walk again, to help us in mobile form!"

"Most certainly. I'll also be able to do something I've wanted to do for a very long time, and just haven't had what it takes."

"Which is?" Penton inquired.

Oliver shook his head wryly. "Get drunk."

"I confess," Turner said, "certain uses of the flesh have not been dimmed by my Godly impersonation."

III: 8

>──◇──◇──◇──◇──◇──◆◄

Darkwing sat with Oliver Dolan beside Geoffrey Turner's van, enjoying a mild spring day. It was clear weather, Styx weather, that made you appreciate not merely Nature around you, but the warmth of Nature within you.

"How are you feeling then, Darkwing?" Oliver said absently, only marginally diverting his attention from an examination of tree buds and the antics of a robin couple.

Darkwing grunted and rolled his eyes sorrowfully. His ribs were wrapped round with bandages concealing the cavity where Vlad Paler's devices had been implanted. His other wounds had been similarly patched, except for the ear that Penton had sewn on. The graft had not taken. "I'll be glad when your Mr. Turner can spend a little more time on this poor body. It's in absolutely wretched condition. This big carcass wears down quick, it does!"

"Yes, well, I think that will be some weeks yet. Turner has to see to fixing himself, you know."

"I don't know if I can make it! Oh, I curse the day I chased that rabbit! I hate myself now. Oh, that I could repent my cowardly ways, and change." The jabberwock breathed a long sigh. "I would have gone through all that again, if I could have avoided killing the girl."

Oliver was quiet for a moment. "Yes. I know what you mean." He looked the beast up and down. "Hmm. As to your state . . . well, I dare say that once the computer facilities are up to snuff again, and Turner's clone is grown, he will be able to give you an overhaul or even a different body, if you like. A phoenix, Darkwing! You can rise from your own ashes. Strike your fancy?"

"I confess, I have grown tired of these ugly features." Darkwing decided not to mention Hampton's loss. Some things are too intimate to bring up with new friends.

"You're not much to look at, true. . . ."

A moment of silence passed, then Oliver nerved himself to ask what he'd been unable to ask before. "Tell me, Darkwing. When Paler killed her—when he used you to push her over the line . . . did she go willingly?"

"I don't bloomin' care to talk about that, mate. It's not a memory I'd care to dwell on."

"I'm sorry. I understand. If you just tell me that much, I'll never bother you on the subject again."

"Very well." The jabberwock closed its great eyes and spoke in a monotone. "At first, when she saw her father talking to her, she came readily enough. I can see in the dark, Oliver Dolan. Need and trust were in her face. Yes, and when she realized her father's face was just a video illusion broadcast by Paler over the tube in my chest, terror and realization came to her. I shall curse these claws that strangled her as long as I wear them. She was a lovely thing, and you should not blame yourself for loving her so." He sighed. "Her last word was 'Oliver.' "

"It *would* be." Oliver looked away. "It was her own fault, you know. If only she hadn't run off, Paler could never have taken her. Stupid little—"

"Please. Let us talk of more pleasant things. I—" Suddenly the eyes lost their awareness. They seemed to stare through Oliver one moment, then glaze over. Great greenish tears dribbled down its mottled face.

Oliver hopped to his feet. "Darkwing, are you . . . What's wrong?"

"We—we must talk more later. If you'll excuse me, I must be by myself for a while, Oliver Dolan. Must think this out."

As the beast waddled off further into forest, Oliver stood and leaned against the van's wood-veneer exterior. *Think.* Yes, he had to do some thinking as well.

Geoffrey Turner was in fine form. He hadn't felt so well in a year and a half. A bit bizarre, having one's consciousness in a box, but then it beat living in Satan's warped Heaven and Hell.

Idly, he explored in greater detail the system whereby Hedley Nicholas controlled his nightcreatures. With the peculiar mechanical vision he had developed during his travails, he examined the frequency synthesizer. This could come in quite handy, he thought.

He twirled a vernier slowly, to see what would happen. . . .

At the head of the long walnut table, beneath a glittering chandelier of delicately spun crystal, Vlad Paler sulked. Before him, untouched, lay an exquisitely prepared dish of lightly curried vegetables. Normally Paler was a vegetarian.

Clasped in his fine hand was a goblet of red wine, which a servant to his right topped off after every sip.

"I suppose you're right, Doctor." He tapped the waxed table top.

Dr. Mendelsohn scraped the last bit of chocolate mousse from the bottom of his dessert cup, and savored it slowly. Then: "Foolishness, Paler. Foolishness. Don't want to go off half-cocked. Can't raise a decent army now, anyway. I know you're angry."

"Furious. I've never tasted defeat like this."

The doctor held out his wineglass to be refilled. "Momentary defeat, dear chap. I've been following your political tactics with the emerging nations, and I must admit, they are marvelous, truly Machiavellian!"

Paler cocked his head a bit, preening. "I'm glad you appreciate their subtlety. Still, my dander is up."

"You will have your revenge, I'm sure. But *not* by hurling hordes of reluctant nightcreatures at Computer Mountain. You must realize the value of worthy opponents. Otherwise your eventual victory will lack flavor. And, as you know by now, to have worthwhile opponents, one must occasionally sacrifice short-term victory."

"A sacrifice! Yes, I believe I see what you mean. Their victory might eventually be used against them. Or at least in our favor."

"Precisely. From all signs, there *is* activity within Computer Mountain. Assuming Dolan and Penton *have* achieved entry—well, it merely insures the fortress's eventual vulnerability. A manse is only as strong as those within."

"Doctor, your association with me has done your mental processes a world of good. You're beginning to think just like me." Paler smiled deviously. "My enthusiasm mounts with each of your words."

He took more wine, feeling positively buoyant—and a touch drunk. This business with Oliver Dolan—why, all that was a mere diversion, a game somehow gone awry. Even now there was the possibility that he could easily recoup his losses, bend defeat to his own purposes. "Doctor," he said. "What is in your cards for this evening?"

"Well, I thought I would just light the old fireplace and settle back with a pipe and a book. Relatives sent along a batch of new stuff from my homeland, and I thought I'd examine—"

"What do you say to a game of chess?"

"Well, now, Paler, you know you're superior."

Paler smiled. "I'll spot you a knight."

"That *would* be intriguing, I must admit. I say, Paler, can't you give it all a rest?"

"Pardon?"

"Must you always be gaming or plotting or controlling this or that. Perhaps you'd like to borrow a few of my books."

"Dear Doctor, haven't you learned yet? In this Universe, it's either control or be controlled. I not only wish to be the captain of my ship, I wish to be the architect, the navigator, the sea itself." He rose imperiously, command in his voice. "Come and play chess!"

The doctor patted his lips politely with a napkin. "Very well."

"Then we must have a short discussion of topics of interest to me." Paler placed an arm around his companion's shoulders in a brotherly fashion as they began to walk toward the gaming chambers. "Of particular concern is the use of that homunculus I extracted from Darkwing. I mentioned before—"

Suddenly Paler stiffened and his complexion darkened. He stumbled, then fell headlong to the floor.

Curious, Geoffrey Turner thought. Such a response was strange on *this* frequency.

He was about to transmit an interrogatory when he was interrupted.

"I say, Mr. Turner. Could I have your attention, please?"

Caspar Penton stood by one of the Einstein's oculars.

"The microchemistry unit's broken the code, I believe! But I need your assistance immediately."

Quite forgetting the tuner and the frequency, Geoffrey Turner focused his attention upon the more immediate problem as Penton switched his power to LOCAL before picking him up for the move to the vat chamber.

"I say, Paler! Not one of your attacks!"

Paler did not respond. There was no pulse, no heartbeat, no sign of breath.

III: 9

OLIVER DOLAN entered and the door slid shut behind him.

"You called for me?" he asked, distracted, eyes unaccustomed to the light. He'd been outside all morning. For the entire week he'd confined himself largely to the outdoors, ambling about the greening countryside.

Caspar Penton looked up from his worktable. "Ah. Darkwing located you, sir."

"How is Turner?"

"Oh, he says that in about three months his half-clone will be mature. The actual grafting can begin. Then he'll be mobile. Not *exactly* as before, he claims, but he seems happy at the prospect."

"I'm glad."

"My goodness, yes. You should have seen the old computer go at these little devils." He tapped one of the blood samples that Oliver had provided some weeks earlier. "Had the thing's genetic code down in a moment, you know. The computer explained it as it worked. Of course, we had to find the proper plasmid to neutralize the parasite's masquerade so that the antibodies could have at them without hurting the host. Fascinating! This computer has magnificent diagnostics!" He leaned back, smiling tiredly. "Of course, it took a while. Deuced clever, this fellow Paler was, with his genetic juggling. I'm afraid that if he's to be the antagonist of the future, we've a rocky road ahead." He picked a test tube from a rack. "But we'll have this! Just a little squirt will do it, sir. The computer showed me how." He picked up a hypodermic needle from a sterilized stainless-steel tray. It was already filled with the clear liquid. "A single squirt, and within an hour, the little devils will be expunged. Totally destroyed. No more vampires! Those now controlled by the disease—the formerly dead—will be at rest. Those yet undefeated presently will have a chance at a normal life. We've done it, sir!"

"Good of you to be so faithful. I'm sure the bonus awaiting you in Fernwold will make it worth your while."

Penton blinked. "Sir. I didn't . . . my friend, I didn't just do it for the money!"

Smiling weakly, Oliver slumped into a chair across the table from his manservant. "No. Not just the money, Penton. I know that."

Penton was nonplussed. "I must admit, that was a factor at the beginning. I'm not entirely a crazy man."

"You've been a brick, my dear friend. I barely know you. We should talk more."

"That would be pleasant. But first, sir, please . . . I've a nice little cotton swab here, and this needle. Just roll up your sleeve, show me a vein, and all of this will be over."

Oliver looked away. "Will it? I wonder."

There was a long silence between them.

Penton sighed. He tried to say something, but could not find the right words. Eventually, he managed to speak.

"Sir. Oliver . . . you risk too much."

Oliver closed his eyes.

"I think I understand," Penton said finally.

"Do you?" Oliver's words were hard and sarcastic.

"Yes, Oliver. I do." Penton took a deep breath, as if trying not to restrain his emotions for once. "Oliver, when infected with the disease, one apparently undergoes a certain—how shall I say it?—transformation. You, for example, had something quite special with Jennifer because of it. Telepathy, Oliver. Empathy. Things are different now, aren't they, sir? You realize that you need people."

Oliver opened his eyes wide. "Penton. How could you?"

Caspar Penton chuckled humorlessly. He rolled back his shirt-sleeve. On his bicep were two tiny scars.

"Oh my God," Oliver said. "Did Jennifer?—"

"No. One of those vampires in the den had a brief go at me. Just a nip."

"And all this time—you've experienced what I've been going through."

"No. Only a bit of it, I think. I hadn't a Jennifer to tempt me."

"Why didn't you . . . Why, we could have talked about it. We could have *helped* each other, Penton!"

Penton shook his head. "We had to do it ourselves, Oliver. No one else can do it for us."

"And you want to take it away from us? These talents, these feelings we know now? Why?"

"You've confused the cause with the effect, Oliver. The parasites are merely catalysts. The need, the potential for these talents, these *emotions*—ghastly word for an English-

178

man, that, but true—were there all the time. Suppressed. Even perverted, by our egos.

"Perhaps if Paler weren't still about, we might experiment with these so-called vampire colonies. But the chap is still kicking about, ready to take you over at any time. And you know, of everybody on this world, I pity him the most."

Idly, Penton dabbed at the crook of his arm with a cotton swab swollen with rubbing alcohol. "Oliver, I've changed with this journey. Winter has turned to spring here in this stiff, proper manservant. I've watched you, poor MacPherson—Jennifer. All of it. I've confronted myself with my own hatreds and evil. And most of all, I've met that part of myself that frightened me the most. My capability to love." He took up the hypodermic needle and pushed out the air bubbles with a squirt. "Before, I was a victim of Victorian society. I saw myself as an unimportant cog in the mechanism of chaos. A product of determinism and existentialism. Now, I'm beginning to see myself as part of something wonderful, a journey from genesis to revelation, repeated over and over. I can't begin to pretend to understand it. But to understand the predicate of that sentence, one must first understand the subject. Who am *I?* I'm beginning to see all life as one, Oliver. I don't have to master understanding or other people or my environment anymore. I just have to accept it." Penton inserted the needle casually. He squeezed the plunger slowly, then pulled the needle out. "The cure isn't going to stop that, Oliver. Not for a moment. I can't make you take this, Oliver. That's your decision. But it will always be here when you need it." He walked to the doorway. "And Oliver," he said, turning around. "I'll always be available, if you need me."

After Penton left, Oliver Dolan sat for a time, thinking. He watched the rhythm of the computer status displays and listened to the hum of machinery, then stood and picked up the hypodermic.

Crickets chirruped in the night.

The moons were both high against the star-mantled sky, like the headlights of an unseen vehicle silently traveling toward some unknown destination.

Oliver paused at the rear door of his vehicle, gazing up for just a moment. The emptiness he sensed above was amply reflected in his own heart. But he felt the stars as well, and the moons and the presence of the sun, some-

179

where behind this planet now, raging and roaring at the vast night.

He tasted the night tastes, the cool and the damp. He felt the night feelings as he had never before felt them. He looked back at the monolithic mountain which hid its bleak corridors of steel and plastic. No, he didn't like sleeping there. He preferred the van.

He listened to a nightbird's song for a moment.

Not a bit of it . . . He didn't even presume to understand a small bit of it anymore.

At least now, though, he knew there was more than just understanding.

Entering the van, he went to the closet to select his nightclothes. Hanging there beside them was one of Jennifer's frocks. Her smell still clung to it, a silent ghost.

Nightclothes donned, he inserted a rock-music crystal into the player. He slipped on the headphones. He turned the volume to just below the threshold of pain. Under the covers, he clutched his feather pillow, waiting for the sleep he knew would be a long time coming.

He left the electric light burning.

EPILOGUE

THE SNOWS had melted. Spring was in the air.

Hampton hoisted himself the final few inches to the lip of the cave mouth. Exhausted, he slumped against cold stone of the mountain while staring glumly at the landscape.

He'd mistimed everything. The climb had taken hours longer than expected and, instead of rising into a cheery dawn, Hampton arose into the red rays of a sun close to setting.

Hampton pulled a piece of dried dragon flesh from his pocket. He'd been living on the stuff for a long time. Some strips he'd frozen, others he'd managed to preserve using the salt crystals so common on the cavern floor. Mostly, though, he had dried the meat over a fire.

Resigned by then to its taste, Hampton chewed the dragon meat mechanically while reviewing his situation.

The long weeks had been trying. Paler's werewolf henchmen had returned to search him out, clearing away the blockage, but he had learned every nook and cranny of the place, and easily eluded them. The hardest part had been the isolation—he was alone in the dimness but could hear soft whirs and mutters from the portal. Occasionally patterns of light would streak the ceiling with color. He'd lose himself in wonder, then, experiencing emotions strange and new. At times Hampton even contemplated his relationship to some type of life beyond that of homunculus to Darkwing.

All the while, the portal beckoned in a strange, undemanding manner.

It had always been his intention to escape the cavern as soon as weather permitted. With the ground free of snow and the air warm, he could venture into the wilderness to relocate his jabberwock.

Now, however, as he looked out upon the land just short of night, the sights and sounds and smells gave him pause. In the distance, he could make out a pair of circling hawks. From the forest, he fancied he heard the rustle of predators. The air held the unmistakable scent of danger.

Small as he was, how long could Hampton expect to

last? And exactly where was he to go? He really hadn't thought *that* bit out.

Hampton remained seated and watched the sun set. Thought of return to Darkwing had sustained the homunculus through the subterranean months, kept him also from falling prey to the portal's siren call. Before, it had merely been a temptation to be fascinated by, yet to turn from. Now, the sudden realization of natural dangers before him, the possible danger of the unknown below seemed not so strong. Its attraction was reinforced.

Suppose he *did* explore the portal. Not for Paler's sake, but for his *own*. If he did survive, if he *did* return—why, then he'd have something to bargain with if Paler came back to the cavern. He had dragon meat enough for months.

What wonders awaited him?

Suddenly, Hampton's commitment to Darkwing seemed not so great. His curiosity and his need for a strange, new kind of fulfillment became much more immediate.

With one more glance out at the surface world, Hampton breathed a sigh. Then he turned his back to the coming darkness and began the journey down to the light in the cavern.

ABOUT THE AUTHOR

David Bischoff was born December 15, 1951, in Washington, D.C. He earned his B.A. (1973) in Radio, TV, and Film at the University of Maryland. He lives in Arlington, Virginia, single with no pets, a full-time writer.

A science-fiction fan since his early teens, Mr. Bischoff has been active in local and national sf functions. At present, he is vice president of the Science Fiction Writers of America.

His passions, besides science fiction, include British television, film, and European rock music.